THE ULTIMATE SIN

TERRENCE D. ASTLEFORD

AUTHOR'S NOTE:
This is a work of fiction. All names, characters, places and incidents either are the product of the author's imagination or are used fictitiously, and any resemblance to actual persons, living or dead, events, or locales is entirely coincidental.

PREFACE

Having met in Kissimmee, Florida in 1997, Terrin and Kensing became fast friends. Once they knew each other for a couple of years, they soon became best friends. While living next door to each other for so long, they decided to move in together and save money. As time wore on, the two became almost inseparable. They would go to the bars together and had a great time. When they went into the bars, they were known as the, "Terrible Two". Walking into the bar one night, a couple of guys came up and started some shit with them. Trying to be nice about it, they were soon in the middle of a fight. Taking a few punches, they beat the two up and run them out of the bar. Being praised and patted on the back, they laugh it off and the bartender gives them drinks on the house, for the rest of the night.

There was one time, when Terrin actually saved Kensing's life. Kensing was working on one of his construction sites when Terrin pulled up. Getting out of his car, Terrin says, "Hey...Kensing.... Duck", as a truss goes sailing towards him. Ducking just in time, Kensing looks up and sees the truss go sailing over his head. Thanking Terrin for saving his life, he decides it is time to quit for the day. Telling the guys to finish setting the trusses, he leaves with Terrin. They also had a few bad times where they got mad at each other, but nothing so bad as to ruin their friendship. They even had a minor dispute over a female one time, but that was the first and last time they fought over a female. They decided it wasn't worth the relationship.

As their lives wore on, things changed… and so did they. Kensing bought his own construction business and Terrin went to night school to become a micro-magnetic engineer. One day while Kensing was on the job site, a careless crane worker who was on drugs, lost a load of trusses. Falling on Kensing, the emergency squad got him to the hospital just in time. Any longer and he would have went into cardiac arrest. Hearing about the accident on his scanner, Terrin rushes to the hospital and waited until he could see Kensing. After getting out of surgery, the doctor said everything was a success and that he should be waking up in an hour or so.

As Kensing's life started falling apart, Terrin dreaded telling him his news. He couldn't tell him that he got a job offer in Colorado. Not this soon after his accident. Deciding to call and postpone his start date, he uses the phone and explains the situation to them. Understanding his plight, they agree to let him start as soon as he can. He only got the job, cause he was the top person in his class. When Kensing finally got released from the hospital, Terrin drove him to the house they were living in. Waiting to tell Kensing for a few more days, he finally tells him that he got a job offer in Colorado with a company called, "KNIGHTWARP Industries", with the starting pay at $100,000 per year after taxes.

Telling him he has to take the job, they say their good-byes. Terrin leaves Florida to go to Colorado. Driving to Colorado, Terrin stops off at a few places to check out the sights, as he knows he may not be seeing much of them in the near future. Enjoying his time alone, he calls the company up on his way and tells them he will be arriving the following Monday ready for work. Having three more days to get there, he knows he can make it in a day or so if he drove all the way through. As his move actually dawns on him, he realizes he still has to unpack his stuff and find his new place to live.

Leaving Topeka Kansas, he heads west on I-70. Driving along, he thinks about the past few years. He laughs to himself as he dwells on all the good times he has had. He can't believe how much his life is about to change. He starts getting nervous as he gets closer to Colorado. He has weird feelings about all this. It's almost like it's a dream. His life is not what he dreamed it would be as a child. He thought he would maybe go to space or write a book. Something that would leave his mark on the world. He couldn't leave this world without leaving some kind of memory. Something that people would remember for ages to come. Maybe he will find some kind of advanced technology that no one knew about.

Who knows? Maybe he will win a Pulitzer Prize for the greatest discovery known to man. He could still leave his mark on the world yet. Looking down he sees he is almost out of gas. Stopping at the next gas station, he barely makes it. Filling up with gas and grabbing a quick bite to eat, he continues on his journey. Getting to Colorado he starts to get really nervous. He gets a little anxious and excited at the same time. And when he starts getting like that, then all you men out there know what happens, if you have ever experienced it before. Driving for hours, he sees hardly anything worth mentioning. Just a lot of open, flat land. Seeing a sign up ahead, he reads it as he goes by: Limon 15

Shaking his head, he makes up his mind to stay there for the night. Arriving in Limon a few minutes later, he pulls up in the first place that has a vacancy. Checking in he goes to his room and takes a shower. Taking care of his exciting problem, he finishes his shower and lies across the bed. Falling asleep as soon as his head hits the pillow, he has weird dreams about things that just don't make sense. Waking up sweating profusely, he turns the air conditioner on. Going back to sleep, he sleeps peacefully the rest of the night.

Waking up the next morning around 8:00 a.m., he takes a shower and gets dressed. Packing his things back up, he goes to his car and puts his things in. Getting in his car, he pulls out of the lot and continues heading west. As he goes down a hill and hits the crest of it, he sees the mountains of Colorado. They are as beautiful as I have always imagined, he thinks to himself. Smiling to himself, he drives forward now. Arriving in Denver at 11:00 a.m., he calls the number they gave him and they send out someone to show him where he lives.

As he waits around, he talks to a few people about Denver. Being curious, he wants to know all there is to know. Seeing a black limo pull up, the window in back rolls down and a gentleman asks if he is the man from Florida. Telling him yes, he gets into his car and follows the men. Taking C-470 heading west, they get off at 285, (Hampden Avenue). Driving back for a few miles, they finally arrive at this really nice house. Getting out of the limo, the guy comes over and hands him the keys and tells him how to get to the facility as he hands Terrin a map. Shaking his head up and down, the guy leaves and Terrin goes up the front steps to the door. Putting the key in, he unlocks the door and goes in.

As he enters, he is in a rather large foyer. Looking up he sees stairs to the left and the right. They curve gradually up and around as they meet at a balcony. Going to the right, he enters the living room or so he guesses. Continuing his inspection of the house, he finds a kitchen and dining areas. He also locates a restroom and a den. Going up the stairs, he finds two huge bedrooms and a study. He also sees that each room has it's own bath. Going back downstairs, he goes into the kitchen and opens the fridge. Seeing that it is turned on and spotless, he is dismayed when he sees an empty fridge. I will have to remedy that really quick, he thinks to himself. Going to a door that he thinks is a pantry; he opens the door and finds a basement. Going down the stairs, he sees a fully remodeled basement with a bedroom and a pool table. He also locates a wet bar, fully stocked too. Making himself a drink, he smiles to himself and feels like his life is changing for the better.

PART 1

1 YEAR LATER

CHAPTER 1

After he got out of the hospital, the doctors told him he wouldn't be able to work any longer. Not coping to well with that idea, he starts getting prescriptions from his doctor. His doctor starts him out on something mild, as the pain isn't all that bad. Going to therapy for weeks on end, he feels he is in a lot more pain and tells his doctor he needs something stronger. His doctor starts prescribing stronger drugs to him. Not really feeling like the drugs are doing him any good, Kensing sets up a small laboratory in his garage out back of his house.

Melissa, who lives across the street, is hoping to major in pharmacology when she gets out of school. When she knocks on the door, Kensing opens it and sees her smiling as she waits to enter. She has blondish brown hair to her shoulders and hazel eyes. When he answers the door he says, "Hi Missy...what brings you over here today?"

"Well... My boyfriend and I just had a fight.... My mom took his side and now I am all upset.

You are the only one I can turn to who will actually listen to me", she says as she starts crying.

"Hey Missy… It will be all right.... Don't worry... Like I always told you, if you need a place to stay or someone to talk to, I will always be here for you", he says as he comforts her.

"I just can't deal with all this right now".

"That's all right... Take it easy... Life isn't all that bad. We all have bad times and people come and go in our lives", Kensing says as he starts remembering how him and Terrin used to be. "Remember Terrin who used to live with me?".

"Yeah... Everyone thought you guys were gay", she says as she starts smiling.

"No... We weren't gay. We were just real good friends who happened to like a lot of the same things. There is nothing wrong with having a best friend to share all your times with. But he left and I haven't heard from him for a year now", as he starts sounding sad.

"Hey... I'm the one who is upset here", she says as she starts laughing at him.

"That's all right... I can be sad too... Besides, we are supposed to be friends and we listen to each other's problems and learn from them", he replies as he starts laughing too.

"Now I see what Terrin saw in you".

"He's the one who made me like this... He is crazy as a lunatic… He is funny, witty and he always has some kind of comeback for anything anyone might say", he says as he starts laughing at some of the memories coming back to him.

Laughing with him, she soon forgets all her troubles. When they finally quit laughing and are getting serious, Kensing asks, "Aren't you into medicines and things like that?"

"Yeah... What do you need?"

"Well.... I have a little lab set up in my garage and I am in soo much pain, I was going to see if we could make some kind of drug that would ease my pain", he says as he tries to get up out of the chair. Wincing in pain as he does, she starts feeling sorry for him.

"Yeah... We might be able to. Besides... This could be really good for me to study on my own and learn things no one else knows in school", she says with a sly smile playing about her lips.

"Cool... I was a little leery not knowing if you would help or not".

"You are my friend... And it's not like we are going to sell it to anyone... I mean it is for personal use only right?" she asks with a serious look on her face.

"Of course it's for personal use. I would never sell drugs to anyone else", he says with a stern look on his face.

"Okay... When do you want to start?"

"Well... What do we need?"

"Here... I will make a list and we will go to the store and see what we can get".

Thinking for a short time, she finally finishes her list and hands it to him. Taking off and going to the store, they get everything on her list. Getting back to his house, they go out to the garage and put things where they need to be. As they experiment and she explains to him what does what and what can't be mixed. Telling him what to do, he does as she tells him and pretty soon they have a really good drug that takes all his pain away and still leaves him in control of his mind.

As they experiment and time goes on, they get obsessed with experimenting. Catching lizards and other small animals and such, (the biggest being a dog), they soon start finding different things that work differently on different creatures. Finding a drug they mixed by accident, they find something that deals with the ESP side of their brains. Finding out only because the dog is the one they injected with it and soon they can start hearing things in their minds. It took them about three weeks to actually put two and two together to understand what was happening.

"I think we have a breakthrough", Kensing says, excitedly.

"I think we have too. I have never heard or seen anything like this", Missy replies as she starts mixing the drug up.

"I wonder if it works on humans like it does the dog", Kensing muses out loud.

"It might.... But the side effects could be... devastating. We know nothing about this yet. Besides, we need a person who is willing to try it out. And as far as I know, I don't know anyone that would be willing to try it".

Smiling at her, Kensing says, "What about me?"

"Wait a minute... No way.... I wouldn't even suggest that", she replies with a serious tone to her voice and the same look on her face.

"But I am the best qualified.... Let's say I took a small sample and we ran tests on it. We can take some of my samples of blood and such and see if it reacts badly with me".

"Well... We can run tests and see if it will harm you".

"Let's do it then", Kensing replies as he starts getting his own samples.

Running tests and analyzing everything, Missy leaves as she has to go home for the night cause she has school the next day. Leaving Kensing to run the rest of the tests, she goes home. After she has gone, Kensing finally notices he is alone and says to himself, the hell with this. Sucking up two cc's of the stuff into a syringe, he puts the needle into his arm and injects it. As he pulls the needle out, he feels funny and starts wobbling. Sitting down in a chair, he rests for a few minutes. Not feeling to hot all of a sudden, he heads into the house where he takes a bath. Getting into the tub after the water is in, he relaxes.

Falling asleep in the tub, he starts having these strange dreams about ruling the world. Waking up four times before he realizes he is in cold water, he gets up and out of the tub. Pulling the drain as he gets out, he goes into the bedroom and falls asleep again. Waking up twelve hours later to someone banging on the door, he gets out of bed and answers it. Opening the door, he sees it is Missy. "Hi Missy", he says, as he starts wobbling again. "I'm not feeling to hot today… Maybe you should go out and finish the tests yourself".

"Okay.... I hope you get better. If I find anything out, I will let you know about it as soon as I can, okay", she asks?

"Okay… Thanks", as he heads for the bedroom.

Going out to the lab, she finds the drug and is about to run some tests when she realizes there are two cc's of the stuff missing. Dawning on her, she goes into the house. Going into his bedroom, she demands to know what the hell he thinks he is doing? Explaining to her he just wanted to see what it would do, she tells him if he ever does that again, then you can find another person to do this for you. Leaving and going back into the lab, she starts running more tests and finds a few flaws that she sees in him now. She finds out that the effect of the sickness should wear off in a day or so. Hoping it doesn't kill him, she starts experimenting with something of her own she has been thinking about a lot lately.

Seeing what her drug will do to the dog, she injects the dog with her formula and writes down what she gave him and when. After the dog has been given the injection, it writhes in pain as it yelps lightly as its body is wracked with fits of convulsions. Hearing the dog talk to her, it asks, what are you doing to me? What have I done to you? Please make the pain go away, it pleads to her as he sends his thoughts. Feeling sorry for the animal, she injects him with a mild painkiller. As the dog starts feeling better, it thanks her mentally.

Looking at her watch, she didn't realize that she had been out here for six hours already. Locking the lab up after putting everything away, she says to the dog, "I will see you tomorrow".

Leaving the lab, she locks the door. Turning around, she comes face to face with Kensing. "Ohhh", she says. "You scared me".

"Sorry... I just started feeling better all of a sudden and now I want to run some more tests and see what I can come up with", he says.

"I ran those tests and as far as I know, you should be all right for now. We still don't know what the long-term effects are yet. I guess we will find out, huh?"

"Good... I will run the other ones and see if I can come up with anything that can predict the long-term side effects. I will pose the question to the computer and see if it can come up with anything", he says as he unlocks the lab door.

"Okay... I will be back tomorrow and I told my mom I was going to spend the weekend with a friend so I can stay all weekend long. If that's all right?" she asks, hesitantly.

"That's fine… That will give us more time to work on these problems. See you later then Missy", he says as he opens the door for her.

"Okay… 'Til later", she says as she leaves and goes home.

Going into the lab, Kensing finds the new drug she was working on. Looking at the dog, he notices something wrong. Going over to the dog he kneels down and starts petting the dog. Not getting any response, he feels to see if the dog is alive. Feeling a pulse he is relieved to know it's not dead. What if it's my drug that did this, he thinks to himself. Is this going to happen to me too, he wonders.

Checking her formula out, he sees she injected somebody or something with it as he finds the syringe with her stuff in it. Nodding his head, he has an idea she gave it to the dog. Taking a sample, he starts running tests on it himself. Seeing the results, he wonders what it will do. What if I mixed hers and mine together and see what the computer can tell me about that. Going over to the computer, he poses the question and it says this configuration will take approximately sixteen hours to calculate. Please wait...

Nodding his head he says to himself, that figures. Continuing with his own tests, he keeps an eye on the dog. Looking up something in a book, he reads it. As the knowledge sinks in, he realizes the drug of his makes you more intelligent. Reading deep into the night, he hears a beep from the computer. Going to the computer, he reads the calculations and smiles. Making a mixture of his drug and hers, he injects himself with just a micron. Going over to the dog, he pets him and checks for his pulse again.

Just then the dog rises and speaks to him mentally. *What's happened to me?*

Speaking back in the same manner, Kensing replies I think she injected you with a thought-provoking drug she was making.

Trying his full capabilities, he commands Kensing to open the door and let him go. Obeying him as if he were the dog's slave, the dog runs out of the yard and down the street. Looking at his watch, Kensing shakes his head and looks around. What the hell just happened, he wonders to himself. Looking for the dog, it is nowhere to be found. "Oh shit", he says as he goes outside and looks for the dog.

Hearing Kensing call for the dog Missy comes out and asks, "What's up?"

"The dog is gone... What the hell did you give him anyway?"

"Just a slight fever reducer with micro-biotic enzymes… Why?" she asks, with a puzzled look on her face.

"Well... It commanded me to open the door and let him go. Whatever you gave him also gave him powers to command other things", he replies with a pissed off look on his face.

"I'm sorry... I thought it would help him cope with his new abilities. I was just trying to help", as she looks down at the ground.

"That's all right. We will just have to improvise. We should get a new subject and see just what your drug will do to it".

"Okay... I have the perfect victim... Errrrr... I mean specimen", as they both start laughing.

"Okay... You go get the specimen and I will set the lab up. I'm going to have to get a cage so we can keep it locked up and have the computer be the only one to open it so it can't influence us".

"Sounds reasonable. We can preprogram times it needs to open. I can set that up".

"So can I. For some reason I have all of a sudden gotten knowledge like never before.

Something is happening... And I like it".

Going in search of her specimen, he heads out and goes to the hardware store for the needed components for the cage.

In Colorado, Terrin is going to work. Transforming the basement into his own private workplace, he starts experimenting with his field of expertise. Setting up switching boxes and field relays, he soon has a better setup than the company. Getting all the necessary metals and screws, he starts working on a platform. When he gets done, the platform is a triangle that is ten feet on all sides. Installing two hydraulic motors on each side, he then proceeds to make three doors that will make a total pyramid when finished. It is exactly ten feet on all sides. Hooking everything up and running cables to the pyramid, he soon has something he thinks can work for what he wants. Trying to develop some kind of platform that can send objects and/or people great distances in a few seconds, he hopes he can make it work.

Running all kinds of fuses and power reducing relays, along with his own power transmitted transformer that can carry 150,000 amps of power in one surge. Hooking up his control panel he has what he hopes is the newest form of transportation. Hitting the go switch, he can hear the power the pyramid is making. Humming like a top, he starts experimenting with buttons to make sure they do what they are supposed to do.

Pushing one button, the sides come down and

the platform then emits high bursts of energy into the air. Crackling like a wild fire, he goes over to the platform and looks at it from all sides. Seeing what looks like clouds but not quite, he can't really make out what it is he is looking at. Looking around, Terrin sees a small red ball on the floor. Going over to it, he picks it up and throws it onto the platform. Disappearing as it goes into the light, he goes on all sides and sees if he can see it anywhere.

Not seeing it, he kind of wonders where the ball went. Snapping his fingers, he thinks of an idea. Turning the system off, he goes out and gets into his truck and heads for town. Going to the nearest animal shelter, he looks at all the dogs and decides on one that looks like it will work. "I'll take that one", he says as he points out the dog. Paying for the dog, he takes it to the store. Getting dog food, he heads home. After he gets the dog inside, Terrin feeds him. After the dog is done eating, Terrin leads him into the basement. Putting the collar and leash on him, he ties the dog to a post. Going over to his control panel, he duplicates his actions from previously and opens the pyramid up.

When the power starts surging, the dog starts whining as it tries to find somewhere to hide. Once the pyramid is opened all the way, Terrin goes over and ties an additional fifty-foot of rope to the leash. Picking the dog up, he throws him into the light. Once the dog is gone, Terrin starts feeding the rope out. Getting to the end, he feels it get taught. Pulling back on the rope, Terrin pulls the dog back out and into the basement.

Wagging his tail and trying to go back into the light, Terrin restrains him. Taking the rope off the leash, he takes the dog over to the control panel, where he closes the pyramid and shuts the thing down.

Taking the dog upstairs, he takes a shower and goes to bed. Having the same nightmares he's been having since leaving Florida, he wakes up a few times during the night. When the alarm clock finally goes off and wakes him up, he realizes it is Saturday. I don't have to work today, he thinks to himself. Getting up, he goes down and makes some coffee. As the water heats up for coffee, he goes out and gets the paper.

Looking at the front page, he sees his company is in the news again. Shaking his head, he can't believe the controversy over what they are doing. We are just trying to make life a little easier, he thinks. Getting into the house, he sets down at the table and lays the paper down. Hearing the coffeepot click off, he makes some coffee and sets down. Reading the lead story, he flips through the paper aimlessly. Coming to the crossword puzzle, he gets a pen and works the crossword.

Once he is done with the crossword, he flips the page and sees the new movies opening up. Scanning down the paper, he sees one he thinks might be good. It is called, "ANNIHILATION FROM HOME". Seeing that it is playing at the drive-in, he decides to go see it. Calling up Tabrinia, he asks her if she would like to go see it. Saying yes, he hangs the phone up and goes into the living room as he turns on the television.

Putting it on the music channel, he gets his laptop computer and proceeds to feed the data on the pyramid into it.

Waiting for the results he finishes his coffee and gets up to go make another one. Coming back into the living room, he looks at the computer and it has an error message; No such computations available at this time. Need more information. Can't finish with the problem you requested. Shaking his head, he feeds the information it is asking for and clicks on ok. Clicking the button, it pops up a message; this may take awhile. Please be patient.

Taking his laptop down to the basement, he hooks it up to his main computer. Turning the voice activation on, he says, "Computer. Calculate these figures at this ratio to these equivalents".

"That requires password identification please".

"Code Alpha38OmegaAlpha345Beta override. Authorization, Terrin7Beta28Alpha64".

"Code accepted. Please wait".

Going to his control panel, he starts marking the buttons and switches. Powering up the system, he opens the sides and powers up the platform. Leaving the system running, he goes upstairs and gets the dog. While he is upstairs, he hears a knock on the front door. Opening it, he sees his assistant, Tabrinia. "Hi Tab".

Looking at him, she thinks he is handsome. At 6'-4" and 190 pounds he is muscular. His hair is brown and shoulder length. His eyes are just the best. Blue but at times they turn to gray. She thinks he has the sexiest eyes she has ever seen. "Hi Terrin... So what are you up to?" as she smiles up at him.

Looking down at her, he sees a rather attractive female at 5'-8" and 120 pounds. She has all the right curves in all the right places. Her hair is blonde and down to her waist. And her eyes are seductive too. They are bright blues, and they just bring out her beauty. "Nothing much. Just testing our system out. I haven't figured out what it does or anything. I just know I sent a ball in and I couldn't see it. So I went to the animal shelter and got a dog. I put the dog in and brought him back. When I started pulling him back, he didn't want to come. He wanted to go back in. I don't understand it".

"Let's go down and take a look. Have you started any computations with the computer yet?".

"I just started them. I should be getting some results back shortly".

"Come on then", she says excitedly as she pulls him by the arm.

Letting her pull him along, they go down to the basement and he shows her what he has done with it. "WOW", she exclaims, as she sees the pyramid. "That is so cool".

"I thought so too. It just came to me and I started hooking things up, but it was like I always knew how to do it".

"Have you went in yet?"

"Nooooo.... Not yet. I want to send the dog in with a camera on its back and see what it can show us".

"Okay... Where's the dog?"

"He’s somewhere upstairs. I was up there getting him when you knocked on the door".

"I will be right back", she says as she smiles at him sexily.

Smiling back, he watches her butt as she goes up the stairs. Looking for the dog, she finally finds it and brings it downstairs. "Found him", she says as she sets him down next to Terrin.

"Cool. Here... Let's put this on him", as he hands her a harness.

Putting the harness on the dog, he sets up a video camera to the dog. Attaching his rope to the leash again, he tosses the dog into the light. As the rope is being let out a little at a time, he gets to the end and starts pulling the dog back. Pulling hard, Tabrinia sees he is having a hard time trying to get the dog to come back so she goes over and helps him. Finally getting the dog back, they take the video camera off the dog and rewind the tape. Hooking it up to the monitor, they play it and what they see amazes even them.

"My god.... It’s a doorway to somewhere else", he says.

"Yeah... But where?" Tabrinia asks.

"I don't know. But wherever it is, I can see why the dog didn't want to come back".

"So... What do we do now?"

"We keep this between us and we will experiment on it. I want to try some different settings and see if it takes us anywhere else".

"Okay", as she looks at her watch. "Hey... We need to get ready. The show starts in an hour and a half".

"Let me power the system down and we'll go".

Powering the system down and closing the doors, they lock the basement up and leave. Driving his truck, they arrive at the drive-in at 6:47 p.m. An hour before the show starts. Finding a place to pull into, they park and go to the concession stand for drinks and eats. Going back to the truck, they put their stuff in and get in. Turning the radio on, they talk and listen to music until the show starts. As the preshow ads come on she says, "I heard about this movie. It's supposed to be the best thriller of the year".

"Really", he says as he raises one eyebrow and laughs.

Laughing with him they watch the show as they eat their popcorn and drink their soda's. Watching as the star gets killed and the others make it out, they see the finish as the rest of the people come ashore and Lewis says, "We did it. We won..."Then they see the screen blank out and three words appear, OR DID THEY?

"I think there is going to be a sequel to it", Terrin says.

"I wouldn't doubt it. But it was an awesome movie. Kind of makes you think if maybe it's not true".

"It's just some crazy guys weird idea", Terrin says as he looks at her with a crazy look on his face. "What about the next one. Have you heard anything about it?"

"I have heard it is supposed to be pretty good. I think it's the same author of the first one. It's suppose to be some short movies".

"All thrillers I suppose".

"Of course. He's the newest master of the macabre. He's the hottest author around right now", she says. "I have all his books. He even did some adult books at one time too", she says as she smiles at him.

Smiling back he says, "So.... He's a good author, huh?"

"The best".

Watching the last movie, they leave the drive-in as the credits are rolling up the screen. Driving back to his house, he unlocks the front door and they go in. Turning the lights on, he asks her if she would like a drink. Saying yes, he fixes them a couple of drinks and takes them into the living room. Setting hers down in front of her, he sits across from her. Talking the night away, they soon have had three drinks each and are starting to feel the effects of them. Going over next to Terrin, Tabrinia sits down next to him, as he tells her a story about him and Kensing.

Enrapt in his story telling, he doesn't pay attention and doesn't realize she is next to him. When he finishes his story, she starts kissing his neck. "Terrin... I can't tell you how long I have wanted to be with you", she whispers as she continues kissing his neck.

"I have wanted you for a long time too", he replies as he kisses her full on the lips.

As their passion overwhelms them, they find themselves upstairs and in bed, making love. Taking lovemaking to a whole new extreme, he shows her just what he can do. As they lay down in bed after their loving, he smokes a cigarette.

"You are the best ever", he says to her.

"No... You're the best", she replies, as she smiles at him and takes his cigarette out of his mouth and takes a drag.

"I fell in love with you when I first saw you", he blurts out.

"Really..... I fell in love with you when you smiled at me that first day. I saw deep in your eyes that you were hurt before and that you were a very open and honest man. I also liked your eyes. They are soooo..... Different".

"Was my pain that oblivious?" as he looks at her with eyes wide.

"To me it was. I don't think everyone picks up on it like me", she explains.

"So... Where do we go from here?" he asks.

"We can leave it at workers or we can be lovers and friends. The choice is yours".

"No. It's our decision. We have to agree on it together. I myself would love to be your lover, friend and co-worker", he confesses.

"Same here", she replies as she smiles at him.

"Then I guess it's settled then. We will be a team. Always", he says as he smiles at her and takes her in his arms.

"Then so be it" as she hugs him back and smiles.

CHAPTER 2

After getting everything he needed from the hardware store, Kensing gets back to the lab. Finding Missy already there, she helps him unload the car with everything. As they build a cage for the animal, Kensing sees it is a dog, but a little bigger than his original. "So… Where did he come from?" he asks pointing at the dog.

"He came from around... There is also a cat here somewhere", she says as she bends down to look for it.

Noticing her sexy body, Kensing gets turned on as he watches her every move. Finding it she brings it up and shows him. "See".

"Yes, I do see", he replies with a sarcastic tone to his voice.

As they both start laughing, they get busy building two shelters for the animals. Once they are done they are satisfied with the results. Putting the animals into their own cages, they both go to the computer and lock out future access to the animals. "I think we can plant a little of the drugs into their food and see if it works as well taken orally", she suggests.

"Okay… Let's do it and see what happens".

Prepping the food, Missy finishes shortly and has the drugs in the food. Meanwhile Kensing is loading the computer up with a series of questions, about how to hook the animals up to the computer, to monitor body functions. Getting the necessary list needed to make it work, he tells her he will be right back. Going to the computer store, he finds almost everything except for some capacitors. Going to the nearest electronics shop, he finds what he is looking for and goes back home.

Going into the lab, he shows her what he got. As they both follow the computers instructions on how to hook it up, they get the monitoring system working. Looking at his watch, Kensing notices it is 6:00 p.m.… "Hungry?" he asks.

Thinking about it for a few seconds, Missy says, "Yeah... What do you have in mind?"

"I was thinking of ordering a pizza".

"Sounds good to me", she replies as she tells him what she prefers on a pizza.

Going to the phone, he calls up the pizza place and orders a pizza, with what she wanted on it. Hanging up, he relates that it will be thirty to forty minutes. "Okay", she replies.

"Computer... Start monitoring system.... Now", Kensing says.

"Starting monitoring system, please wait", the computers voice says. "Calculating time to known effects...................... Fourteen hours, thirty-nine minutes and twenty-four seconds ‘til completion on analysis".

"Start calculating then", Kensing says as he

sounds a little irritated.

"Calm down", Missy says. "It's only a computer. It can only do so much".

"I know. It just pisses me off sometimes, telling me stupid facts and figures. I just can't get over the technology we have created. We would all die without power. We rely on power far too much", he states.

"What does that have to do with this?" she asks feeling slightly confused.

"I don't know. I must be rambling on", he says, shaking his head.

"That's okay... We all do that", as she smiles at him.

"I just happen to do it more than others... huh?" he asks as he starts laughing.

Laughing with him, she replies, "Maybe".

"Oh..... I see", he replies sarcastically.

"No... Not like that", as she laughs harder.

Getting control of themselves, they start watching everything to make sure it works right. Checking all the monitors, Missy sees slight fluctuations in the kitty's heart and regulatory rate. "I think something's happening to the cat", she says.

Checking the monitors himself, Kensing says, "Okay... We have subject two going to mental capacity".

"It's starting stage two, mind development", she says.

Going over to the cat, he sees the cat's eyes moving about rapidly as if it were in REM. Watching the cat carefully, it suddenly jumps up and meows. "Crazy cat", Kensing says as he suddenly gets the idea of trying to open the cages.

"Poor… Poor cat. Sorry, but we can't even get you out of there. Only the computer can and it's not allowed to. There is no manual override or any access allowed by anyone. The cages will open in about two years and fourteen hours and twenty-six minutes. Nothing can be gained by trying to get out. If you think of killing us, then you will die a horrible death. Cause there won't be anyone to feed you", Missy says, as she talks to the cat.

Jerking her head, the cat answers her, *so I am trapped here for awhile, huh? Well... I will have to figure something out. I can't stay in here forever. I would die.*

"I wouldn't let that happen. We just want to see what this drug does and if there are any side effects. As you probably know, Kensing has injected even himself with the same drug. And he's not trying to hurt you. We want to have better communications with other things", Missy explains.

But you are hurting us by keeping us prisoners. I have never done anything to you. Have I?

"No... But you have gotten me in trouble a couple of times when you knocked the trash can over. And you got me in trouble when…" as she gets cut off.

Okay. Okay. I get the picture. So... When the doors do open, can we go free then? the cat asks.

"Sure. We only need you for that period of time. After that, you are as free as you want to be", she says.

Agreed, the cat replies.

"Have you always had thoughts like this. I mean... Like a humans?"

No. It just all of a sudden happened as if I did have it all my life. Why?

"I am just curious. So it gives you thoughts like our own so we can understand each other", she says as she starts smiling. "Kensing... I think we have a break through. This drug also gives them human thoughts".

"What are you talking about?" he asks a little confused at her outburst.

"I was just talking with the cat and it says it gave it thoughts like ours. Human. So we can understand each other", she says with a look that says, you know.

"I see… Anything else that you know of?"

"Not right now. I suggest further testing", as she turns to the cat and asks, "When the dog can reach your ability, tell him not to try anything cause it won't work. Tell him that if we can cooperate with each other, we will let you go when the doors open. Okay?"

Sure. I will explain it to him and I think he will cooperate. And thanks for being so honest.

"What reason would I have to lie to you. You can read my thoughts. I can't hide from you", she says as she starts to smile.

None. Just checking.

Going over to the monitors, she looks and sees if anything has changed for the dog yet.

Noticing a faint but slight fluctuation, she says, "The dog is going into stage one........ Hold over for the second stage....... Entering stage two..... Coming around.... Now... Okay cat, do it", she says.

Watching as the cat makes weird expressions with its face, they can tell it is talking to the dog. Coming up next to her, he asks, "Want to know what they are saying?"

"You know what they are saying?" she asks, looking at him strangely.

"Yeah. The cat's telling him to lay off trying anything funny, cause he already tried and found out things, the hard way. Now he's forewarning him and telling him that they will be free, as soon as the doors open. He's telling him to cooperate and things will be better", he says.

"Wow... I didn't think you could do that", with an amazed look on her face. "Can you tell me what I am thinking right now?" she asks smiling sexily.

"You are thinking of making love to me as I make love to you. You want me soo bad, but you are scared. You don't know if you are in love or lust. You are confused, but you think you want me. You don't know what to do?" he asks.

"Yeah.... That’s exactly it. But how..."

"Remember... I took some too?"

"Oh yeah... I forgot. Sorry".

"That's all right. You don't have any reason to be sorry for", he says as he looks at the monitors. "I want a little more. I feel a need for more", as he heads for the formula.

"Kensing... No", Missy says as she runs over

and keeps it from him.

"Missy... Don't make me use my powers to get that. I just want a small dose", he says.

"How small?"

"Just a micro-gram. That should be sufficient until the next time. There's one side effect we just found. It's very addictive. Now we need to find an antidote to keep the dependency down".

Drawing up a micro-gram of formula, she injects it into his arm. Pushing the plunger all the way down, she withdraws the needle from his arm. "Better?" she asks.

"Yes", he breathes as his body quivers slightly as he feels the rush hitting him hard.

As he moans in pleasure, she takes the rest of the formula and hides it. Opening his eyes, he says, "Okay, where were we?"

"We were just running some tests on the animals, to see if they have an addiction to this drug too".

"Get me three cc's of morphine-based tranquilizer compound and two cc's of opium-based carbonics. Hurry. These thoughts don't last that long", as he writes down what he can of the formula.

Getting him what he needs, he mixes up the stuff into precise measurements. Finishing it he says, "Place this over the Bunsen burner for five minutes. Then cool off quickly and put into patch form", he says.

"What does it do?" she asks, curiously.

"It will take this drug to a new level that doesn't require addiction. It is a patch that you can wear and you change them every six months. Each patch has just enough to get you by with. That's the best I could think of at the time", he says as he shrugs his shoulders.

"Okay. Let's try it. Maybe then you won't be so edgy all the time", she replies.

When Sunday morning comes, they are in bed sleeping soundly. All of a sudden, they hear a banging coming from downstairs. Getting up, Terrin goes downstairs and sees the dog trying to get into the basement. It was banging its head into the door. "Hey... What's wrong little fella", he says as he bends over and picks him up. Petting him he tries to calm him down. "It's all right" Terrin coos as he pets the dog. Taking the dog upstairs with him, he goes into the bedroom and tells Tabrinia about what the dog was doing.

"Maybe he's trying to get back down there cause that is what he truly wants".

"Maybe. C'mon. Let's get some coffee and do a little research", he says as he swats her bare ass.

"Hey… Hey… Hey.... None of that now", she says, as she starts laughing.

Getting up, they both go downstairs and get their heads together. Making the coffee while Terrin gets the paper, Tabrinia decides to make a little snack. Baking up some eggs and toast, she has breakfast ready by the time coffee is done. Smiling as he comes back in he looks up and says, "You are the best. How did you know I was hungry?"

"Because I am too", as she smiles back at him.

Setting down to breakfast, he says, "The companies in the papers yet again. I'm beginning to think I should just pack up my experiments and take them out of here. If the company gets shut down, then I will lose all this stuff. Let's go into town after breakfast and get a big truck and haul this away somewhere else. I have enough money to keep us going until I can get a job. How about it?" he asks, with sad eyes.

"Okay… I don't have anything holding me here. My job isn't like the best in the world", she says as she starts laughing.

"Good. Then when we are done, we will get a rental truck and pack up all this extra stuff. You wouldn't happen to know of any out of the way places we could rent for awhile. A place where there aren't a lot of people", he says.

"I know. A place called Vaughn, Alabama. I grew up there for awhile and there aren't a whole lot of people and the rent out there is cheap. And.... No one would ask any questions", she says as she smiles.

"Great", he replies as he finishes his breakfast. "That was a great meal babe. Thanks".

"Anytime", she replies.

Lighting up a cigarette, he relaxes for a little bit. After he is finished, he gets up and asks Tabrinia, "Are you ready?"

"As ready as I'll ever be", she says as they head out to the truck.

Heading into town, they drive around for about an hour before they find a place that's open. Pulling into the lot, Terrin and Tabrinia go in and ask one of the clerks if they have a big truck they can rent. Saying yes, they start filling out the necessary paperwork in Tabrinia's name. "I'm just helping her move", Terrin offers, as he backs away.

"How long you want it? One-way or local?", the man asks.

"Ummm..... One way to Vaughn, Alabama", she says.

"Okay… That's one way to... Let's see....... The closest dealer we have there is in Bay Minette. Fifteen miles southeast of there. Is that okay?" he asks.

"Sure. That would be great", she smiles as she shakes her head.

"Okay... Let's see... That'll be twelve hundred and forty seven dollars and sixty-eight cents. Do you have a credit card?"

"Oh yeah... Here", as she hands him her credit card.

Running her card through, it comes back accepted. Handing her the keys he says, "She's the one over by the fence", as he points it out.

Going over to it, Terrin looks at it and says, "It'll work. Let's go. I want to get done before tonight".

"Okay", she replies as she gets into the truck and drives it back to his house.

Pulling into the driveway, Terrin backs up to the basement access. Stopping the truck and shutting it off, he gets out and opens the rear doors. Pulling the ramp out, he opens the basement doors. "Tab. C'mon", he says as he goes down stairs.

Getting down there, he starts by unplugging everything and rolling the cords up neatly and ties them up. Removing the doors from the pyramid, he starts taking things out to the vehicle. Once they have the basement cleaned out, they start taking only the things that are his. Leaving everything else behind, they leave the house and head out of town to Tabrinia's place. Once at her apartment, they get all her things loaded up into the truck also.

Finishing loading her stuff up, they head for Vaughn, Alabama. Pulling over only to get gas and sleep they arrive in Vaughn, Alabama two days later. Letting her lead him around she pulls into a realtor's office. Going in he gets out of the truck and follows her. As they go into the office, they see a rather drab and dull looking office. They see a small woman sitting behind a desk filing her nails. Looking up the woman says, "Can I help you?"

"Yes. We are new in town and are looking to buy a small house with a basement. You woiuldn't happen to have anything like that out in the woods anywhere. We don't like to live near people", Tabrinia says, as she smiles at the woman.

"I think we do. Let me see....... Here we go. It's a lovely three-bedroom house with a full basement and full attic. We have it up for ten thousand, but if you make a cash offer, I am sure we can work something out", the woman smiles at them and they see the lipstick on her teeth.

"How about seventy five hundred", Terrin says, pulling some cash out of his pocket.

"Sure. You just have to sign some papers and then I'll take you to your new home", as she gets all the necessary papers together.

Once all the papers have been signed and the cash given to the woman, she takes them out to the house and shows them the whole property. "It comes with three ponds and forty seven acres. Beautiful country if you ask me", the woman says.

"Well, thanks a lot. It's been nice doing business with you", Terrin says as he shakes her hand and hurries her on her way.

"Okay. If you need anything at all… I mean anything. Don't hesitate to call", she says as she backs out of the drive and leaves.

"Whew.... What a nightmare! Let's check it out", Terrin says as he grabs Tabrinia's ass playfully.

Jumping forward as he pinches her ass, she turns around and playfully slugs him in the arm as she laughs. Going inside they find an old musty place. Cobwebs linger in the corners of the room. There is a fireplace that looks like it hasn't been used since the civil war. Checking all the windows and the floors out, it seems to be a well-built house. Finding the access to the basement, Terrin goes down as Tabrinia follows him. Looking around they see cobwebs and spiders everywhere.

Clearing a path as he goes in, Terrin looks around and visualizes what this place can look like when it's all cleaned up. "C'mon... Let's go get the cleaning things and get this place in livable shape", he says as he heads back upstairs.

Following him up she goes out to the truck and gets her cleaning supplies they got on the way down. Going back in with an armful of stuff, he gets everything else they need to finish cleaning. "Hey babe.... I'm gonna hook the generator up to the house for now. At least we'll have power", Terrin says.

"Okay honey... I'll start in the basement", she says, as she heads downstairs.

Going to the back of the big truck, he opens the back doors and climbs in. Using his hand dolly, he hauls the generator to the edge of the truck and gets down. Going up front, he starts the truck up and pulls the PTO knob up. Engaging the hydraulics, he goes to the back of the truck and uses the knobs there to open and raise the lift gate. When the gate gets up to the top, he climbs up and rolls the generator onto it. Taking the lift down, he goes up front and kills the engine.

Rolling the generator to the electrical hook-up, he wires his two main feeds in and starts the generator. As it starts on the first pull, he waits a couple of minutes before switching it over to the house. As he switches it over you can hear the drain it has on the generator. After a couple of minutes, the generator picks its speed up and continues running smoothly. Seeing a door in the ground, Terrin goes over and opens it up. Looking down inside, he sees what looks like some kind of bomb shelter. Going down the stairs he looks around and thinks to himself, this would be perfect for a lab. I could hide the doors and set everything up down here.

Going back up the stairs he goes into the basement of the house and tells Tabrinia what he found. Going with him, he shows her what he is talking about. Nodding her head in agreement, they start cleaning up the bomb shelter. After what seems like hours of cleaning, the room is finally ready for all the equipment. "Why don't you make something for dinner and I will start getting everything down here and set up. Okay", he asks as he sees a slight smile cross her lips.

"Okay... Things will get better... I know", she says as she gets up and heads for the house.

Going out to the truck, Terrin starts unloading his equipment and taking it down into the new lab. By the time she has dinner made, Terrin has the platform and the control panels setup and ready for business. Bringing the dinner down to the room, he smiles and thanks her for helping him out. Smiling as if she were shy, she smiles back and tells him how much she appreciates his taking an interest in her.

CHAPTER 3

Watching in horror as she sees her mother killed by a car of kids driving by, Tanya is in shock as she sees this. Not believing what she is sees happening she runs over to her mother and says, "Mom ... NOOOOOOO", she yells out. Cradling her mother's limp form, she cries as she holds what is left of her mother. When the cops and paramedics arrive, the police call social services and send for a car. When the social worker gets there she asks Tanya, "Do you know where your father is?"

Shaking her head, she mumbles no.

"Do you know where he lived at all?"

Nodding her head she says, "He lived in Florida, as far as I know" she says as she starts crying again. "Can I go in and use the bathroom?" Tanya asks.

"Sure darling. Go right ahead".

Going into the house, she finds her mothers money stash and takes it. Grabbing her backpack with some clothes in it, she sneaks out the back and runs away. Running until she can't run anymore, she sits down next to a tree and catches her breath. Getting back up, she knows she has to find her father. Heading to the nearest bus station, she finally gets to one and asks how much for a one way ticket to Kissimmee, Florida. Paying the lady she takes her ticket and waits for her bus.

When her bus finally arrives, she gets on and slinks down in the seat. Pulling her jacket over her head, she acts like she is sleeping. Falling asleep and seeing her mother get killed over and over is just too much for her to bear. Waking up she looks around and asks the lady behind her, "Excuse me ma'am. Where are we?"

"We are in Alabama dear. Why?"

"Oh. Just curious. Thanks".

As the bus pulls in for a stop, Tanya gets off the bus and heads for the washroom. Going in she does her duty and cleans up. Going back outside, she sees the bus leaving as she comes out. Hitting her hands against the wall in frustration, she starts walking down the road. Sticking her thumb out, she decides she might as well hitchhike. As a truck flies by her, it stops and backs up. As the window rolls down, a guy asks, "Can I give you a lift to somewhere?"

"Yeah. I just missed my bus and I am looking for my father. I was going to Florida to see if I could find him", she says as she starts crying lightly.

"It's all right. What's his name, if I'm not being too nosy?"

"Terrin Harper", she says.

Just then the truck comes to a very fast stop. Looking at her he smiles and says, "Tanya".

"Dad", she says as new tears flow down her cheeks.

"What happened?" he asks.

"Me and mom were outside, when some guys drove by and shot her", she says. "I saw it all".

Hugging her he says, "Your safe now baby. I will take care of you", he says as tears well up in his eyes.

Going into town, he picks up the things Tabrinia wanted and heads back to the house. Making small talk along the way, they arrive at the house and she says, "Wow... You have been doing real good", she says in amazement.

"No... I have just been working my butt off, so I can get where I am at today. I had to give a lot up".

Going inside he says, "Tabrinia darling... Look who I found walking down the road".

Looking at her she says, "She's a little young... Don't you think?" she asks.

"Tanya... This is Tabrinia. Tabrinia.... This is my daughter Tanya", he says as he introduces them.

Getting that out of the way, she prepares to make dinner while Terrin and Tanya go out and sit on the porch swing and get caught up on their lives. As the aroma of dinner wafts out to them, they both say, "Mmmmmmm", at the same time. Laughing as they say it, they both are in hysterics as Tabrinia comes outside and says, "Dinners ready you two".

Going inside, they all sit down and eat dinner. While small talk goes on, Tabrinia asks Tanya all kinds of questions regarding her knowledge.

Answering all her questions better than she could, she is impressed with her smarts. "Tanya... Have you ever heard of micro-magnetic engineering?" Terrin asks.

"Yes. I think I read an article on it and who actually discovered it. It is actually, a fascinating topic, if you really want to get into it", she states rather smartly.

"That is my field of expertise and the person you read about was me, but I was using a fake name at the time. I had a lot of problems and didn't need anyone finding me. I did do some undercover work at one time", he explains to her.

"Cool. My dad, the smartest man in the world", she says as she beams at him.

"No... I just thought there would be a use for it and I have found the perfect use. I want to show you what we have been working on", he says as he gets up. "Ready to see our project?" he asks as he holds his hand out waiting for her to take it.

Putting her hand in his, she lets him lead her outside to a set of doors in the ground. Opening the doors he leads them down and then tells her, "Close your eyes".

"Okay".

"Don't open them until I tell you to. Okay?"

"Okay", she says a little impatiently.

Turning the lights on he says, "Okay. You can open them now".

Opening her eyes, she sees his experiment and gapes in awe at it. “You've made an electrically charged micro-magnetic power grid".

"What did you call it?" Terrin asks stunned

that she knows what it is and he doesn't.

"Yeah… It's an electrically charged micro-magnetic power grid. It turns small amounts of power into ten times what they were to begin with. It makes power companies obsolete", she says trying to sound knowledgeable.

"No... It's a doorway to somewhere. We can't figure it out yet. But we are working on the problem".

"What do you mean...... Doorway?" Tanya asks incredulously.

"It goes somewhere… But as to where… We don't know yet".

"How do you know it's a doorway?"

"Because... We kind of sent a dog into it and he didn't want to come back", he explains.

"Anything else?"

"Yeah... We have a little bit of footage from when we strapped a video camera to its back. What we saw… We couldn't tell what it was", as they explain to her what they have done and checked on.

Telling her everything they know and showing her all the data on the matter she says, "I can't seem to figure out where it goes to either. But you are right about it being a doorway though. I can see that as plain as day", she says as she points to what she is talking about and telling them what certain things mean on the charts.

Re-computing the figures the way Tanya told them to enter them, they wait and see what the computer will tell them. Looking at the pyramid, she says, "So..... You figured this all out. Cool. I have thought of building something like this in a dream once. But I never thought I would actually ever see it".

"Me either. I thought it was a dream that would never come true", he explains to her. "I remember you in my dream. You walked in on me and I was just walking through the doorway, when you pulled me back out of it".

"Yeah… I remember that. It's all coming back to me now", she exclaims, as she remembers.

"I think for some reason… We have been given this chance and had the same dream for a particular reason".

"But what is the reason... And why did they kill my mom?" she asks as she starts to cry.

"I can't guess, but from what you have told me, she is on some kind of drugs and that might have led to her getting killed. Other than that… I can't guess", Terrin says as he tries to sound intelligent.

"Maybe.... From what I remember, she was always doing some kind of new thing with everyone else around where we lived. But why shoot her?"

"Because… They might have figured she might have seen something or owed them a lot of money she couldn't pay back. I know how those guys are. I have had to deal with them a few times myself… Mind you not for drugs either. I needed their assistance in finding something I needed and they helped out and I gave them what I promised them. Other than that… They usually don't kill anyone. Wait a minute..... Was there anyone else around at the time?"

"Well... There was Marcos and Paul".

"Then they might have been the target and your mom got in the way. If that's the case, then I can have it checked out. I will make some calls tomorrow and see what I can find out... Okay babe?" he asks with tears in his eyes. "Regardless of what anyone says, I have always loved your mom Tanya. She didn't want me", as he breaks down and starts to cry slightly, before he composes himself.

"She always said you were the right man for her... But that she didn't want to take the chance of any break-ups again. She said she wanted to try something different for a change", she said.

"Well anyway. I will look into it and have it checked into without raising any suspicions. I have a few contacts there that I have been using to keep track of you", he admits. "I had to do something to make sure you were all right. I love you more than you will ever know Tanya. I have always thought about you and wished things had been different .You will never know how much I truly missed you", he says as he tries to explain why he had them watched.

"I understand. I always had your picture up in my room.... When I looked at it, I always wondered what you were doing. I was hoping someday we could be together again... But not like this", as she starts sobbing openly and he hugs her and comforts her in her time of need.

Completing all the necessary mixtures, they finally have a patch ready for implementation. Taking one off its piece of plastic, Kensing lifts his shirt up and slaps it on his arm. Feeling a slight rush he grabs hold of the table and steadies himself. "Wow... What a rush", he says as he sits down.

"It gives you a rush, huh?"

"Yeah.... But it's not as bad as the injection".

"Oh... I see... We should have stayed with the injections then, huh?" Missy says as she starts laughing.

"Yeah right", he replies as he laughs with her.

"Okay… I want to increase the dosage the animals are taking and see if the effects are the same, or if they may be different".

"Okay. Let's get started then. We have a lot of work to do before I will be allowed to come back if my mom finds out I have been over here", she says.

Getting all the necessary dosages put into the food, they give it to the animals that sense something is up, but they can't read her thoughts as she is blocking them somehow. Trying to sense something from Kensing, they can't read his mind as he is more powerful and has found out how to block all thoughts from others. When the animals don't touch their food Missy asks the cat, "What's wrong?"

You have done something different to our food. What have you done and why?

"We have only given you a slightly larger dose than usual. Once you get accustomed to this dose, you will feel no other side effects as far as we know".

Okay… So long as that is all. If there is something not right with it, I will kill both of you.

"There is nothing to worry about. What would

we gain if we tried to kill you? Nothing! Except a dead animal. So there would be no point to it".

Very well… I believe you. You haven't lied to me yet, as far as I can tell, so I guess I have to trust you for now. If I catch you in anything other than the truth, then I will kill you, as I have promised, the cat replies, as it starts eating.

"Very well... But if you keep saying you are going to kill us, I will make sure that you die a horrible death, which the computer is programmed to execute....... If something goes wrong", she explains to the cat.

Turning away, she walks over to where Kensing is and sees what he is doing. Looking over his shoulder, she sees he is setting up the next set of tests to be taken from the animals. Helping him get them ready, they hear a knock at the door. Going over to answer it, Kensing opens the door and says, "George... What brings you over here?"

"Well.... We got a call from some people… Who think you are making drugs in your garage. They complained of a weird smell coming from your place and I said I would check it out".

"No... We are running some tests on these two animals. We have come up with a really new kind of drug, that allows other animals and such to communicate with us. Watch", as he tells the cat to get into his head and see what he has planned for them.

Obeying, the cat tells George, *what would it take for you to believe I am the cat talking to you. I got it. Come over here and whisper something that only I can hear and I will repeat it in your head.*

"Okay", as he walks over to the cat and whispers something into its ear.

As the cat repeats what he said, he is awe struck. "I can't believe this. You have come up with something that will let us communicate with animals. This has got to be a tremendous break through. When are you going to tell someone?" he asks, as he seems to get all excited.

"We can't, until we figure out how to make it without the addiction it has. We haven't been able to get rid of that one thing. Other than that, we have had no side effects worth mentioning".

"Cool. So... What do I tell all the guys outside?" he asks.

"Nothing. When you go back outside, you will find yourself all alone. Everyone has left and has forgotten anything ever happened here. As the same will happen to you when you leave", Kensing says. "Sorry brother, but I can't have this getting out just yet".

"So... You are going to mess with my mind when I start to leave?"

"Only to make you forget anything about our little experiment here".

"How can you not trust me. I'm your brother?"

"I can't trust anyone except the person who has been here since the start", he says as he looks over at Missy and smiles.

"Then I will have to make sure you don't mess with my mind then. I won't allow you to manipulate me, like you do everyone else", he says as he pulls his gun out.

"There's no need for that. But if you really

want to use it... I can accommodate you", Kensing says as he gets into George's mind and tells him, when you get to the station, you will kill four officers and then yourself and you will forget about anything that happened here. "You can go now", Kensing says as they shake hands and George leaves.

Getting into his patrol car, he heads for the station and proceeds to carry out the command he was given. Entering the station, he pulls his piece out and kills four of the officers on duty and then sticks the gun in his head. Seeing what is happening, a rookie grabs his arm and pulls it away from his mouth, as it discharges. Fighting with him, he finally gets the gun away from him and manages to cuff him.

While officers and EMT crews are gathering up the dead and injured, they take George into a room and question him endlessly. As they get enough information from him to know that the last place he was, was at his brother's house, they send out a swat team to go over there and arrest him.

When the team pulls up and surrounds his place, Kensing can feel something not right. Sending out his special talents, he finds out that a swat team is surrounding his house. Using his talents, he tells them that they are at the wrong house. As they go and bust into the wrong house, Kensing and Missy collect what they can and start to leave. "Wait... We have to take the animals with us. If we don't, then they will take them and put them through a shitpile of tests", she says.

"Okay... I can only hold off the police for so long before they send in someone that actually makes it past and blocks my thoughts. Let's go down and rent a truck and put everything in it we can", he says as they get ready to leave.

Just as they are about to walk out the door, the phone rings and he picks it up, "Hello".

"Kensing? Is that really you", a familiar voice asks.

"Terrin", he asks with amazement in his voice. "Where the hell are you?"

"I'm in Alabama. I had to leave, as the company I was working for started getting a bad rap from the press and they were out to crucify anyone involved. That meant me too. So... I kind of left and came here to the boondocks".

"Well.... I kind of have the same problem... Except mine has to do with the cops and that they are after me right now. Is there anyway... I.... Or we can come up there and stay with you for a short time?"

"Sure... What are best friends for if they can't help each other out in their time of need?"

"Okay... We are going to rent a truck and be up there as soon as possible. Don't tell me where you're at, exactly. Once I get there you know my beeper number. Page me the day after tomorrow and I will call and we will meet somewhere safe", Kensing says.

"Okay... Nice talking to you again Ken. See you in a couple of day's buddy... Hey, I love you like a brother man", Terrin says as he gets ready to hang up.

"Okay. See you shortly... And I love you too

man. See you later buddy", Kensing says as he hangs the phone up.

"So... Do you want to go with me, or stay here and answer all kinds of questions and possibly give away our location?"

"I can't go. I have to stay here. What about my mom?" she asks thinking about her family.

"Well... Do what you have to. Just don't tell them anything at all. Just give them very little and that all you knew about, was our one experiment and that is all... Okay?"

"Okay. So... Are we going to get a truck or stand here and wait for them to come after us?"

"Okay... Let's get going", as he locks up the lab and they leave.

Finding a truck rental center, they rent a truck they figure should be good enough for the trip up there. While they are getting the truck Kensing is brainwashing Missy into thinking she really wants to go with him.... No matter what... By the time they get the truck and back to his house, they get everything loaded up and his car on a tow dolly. Getting into the truck, Kensing says, "Well... It's been nice working with you Missy. You take it easy and don't forget me", he says as he starts the truck up.

"What are you talking about. I'm going with you", she says as she goes around and gets into the passenger side of the truck.

"Don't worry about me... I just seem to forget soo much lately", he says as he smiles secretly to himself.

As they pull out of his driveway, he sends out subverbal signals to her mother and tells her to forget all about her daughter. You're daughter died two years ago, in an auto accident. Believing what he puts into her head, she goes about her regular routine and never even thinks about her daughter.

Heading to Alabama they are soon having a great time, playing games on the road. Stopping at a motel once Kensing gets a room for them and they go in. Putting their clothes on the rack provided for suitcases, he gets naked and starts the shower up. Hearing the shower she feels like she needs one too. Getting undressed she enters the bathroom and joins Kensing in the shower. Smiling, he starts kissing her and they eventually make their way to the bed.

Making love to each other, they fall asleep after about thirty minutes. Waking up the next morning, they get all their stuff packed and turn the key in. Filling up with gas before they get on the Interstate, they make it to Alabama and wait at a restaurant for Terrin to beep him.

CHAPTER 4

After calling Kensing up Terrin went back to his shop and started working on the configuration for the platform. Sending the dog back in again with the video camera mounted on its back, they tethered it to a fifty-foot rope and tossed him in. After a couple of minutes the dog came running back out. When the dog came through, something came with him. Going over to the power panel, Terrin shuts the system down. As soon as the system starts shutting down, they hear a guttural roar as whatever tried to come through with the dog, got sucked back into the pyramid.

"I can't figure what's wrong... The dog has never done that before..... And whatever tried coming through, never tried before either. I just don't understand it", Terrin says as he scratches his head.

Poring over all the documents he has made and all the data he has collected on the experiment, they all try to figure out what changed. Spending hours down in the lab,

Tabrinia asks, "Anybody hungry?"

"Yeah... I'm starved", Terrin and Tanya say at the same time.

Looking at each other, they start laughing, as if they had a private joke she knew nothing about. Continuing on with the search, Tanya says, "I may have found what you are looking for.... If my information is correct... But I see what you missed", as she hands him the papers.

Taking the proffered papers, he looks at them and smacks himself in the head. "What am I, stupid or something... I forgot to bring my micro-magnetic power bypass coupler dishes".

"You actually forgot something", she says as she starts laughing.

"Hey... Everyone forgets something now and then. Plus, we were in a hurry. I'm surprised I didn't forget a few more things".

"We could run into town tomorrow and get what we need to finish this project. You are supposed to beep Kensing the day after tomorrow. So we have time to go and get what we need", she says as she bites her nails.

"Stop that", he says pointing at her nails.

"I'm sorry... It's a bad habit I picked up, when I was always nervous when mom had her druggie friends over".

"Well.... You won't have to put up with that kind of thing anymore", he replies as he smiles and hugs her.

Double-checking everything to make sure nothing is left on, they leave and lock up the lab. Heading into the house, Tabrinia comes out on the porch and says, "Ohh... I was just coming to get you for dinner", as she smiles at Terrin.

"We can't do anymore till I get some equipment I need. Tanya there, found the problem... We kind of left a couple of things back in Colorado. Of course, if we weren't in such a hurry, we probably never would have forgotten them", he states as he smiles and shrugs.

"Don't tell me... We forgot the dishes for the energy pulses?"

Nodding his head up and down, Terrin says, "You hit it right on the nose".

"I'm sorry... I should have reminded you", as she looks down at the floor.

"Hey.... We were in a hurry... It's both our faults... How could we have known?"

"We just should have. I can't believe we forgot something that important", as she shakes her head.

"That's water under the bridge. We are going tomorrow to pick up the things we need. If you want, you can come with us?" Terrin replies, as he looks at Tabrinia.

"I would like that. Oh... By the way... We need to get a few things from the store. I want to make you guys something special for dessert tomorrow".

"Sure. I needed to get a few things myself anyway. What about you kiddo. Anything special you need or want from the store?"

"Just girl things", she says as she smiles shyly.

Finishing dinner off, they all go out and relax on the front porch, where Terrin lights up a smoke. Looking at the sky and wondering where his doorway takes them, he falls asleep. Gently shaking him, Tabrinia finally gets him awake enough to go into their bedroom. Falling on the bed, Tabrinia takes his clothes off. After getting him undressed, she turns him over and starts doing things to him. Having sex with him when he is sleeping, is not the same, she thinks, as she finally comes to orgasm.

Crawling up next to him, she puts her arm over his chest and falls asleep. As Tanya tried going to sleep, she only dreamed of her mom getting shot over, and over. Waking up, she looks at the clock and sees it is only three-thirty. Getting up, she goes out to the lab and sees if she can get in. Looking at the lock, she goes inside and finds the key to the door. Going back out, she unlocks the door and goes down the stairs.

Looking around, she feels for a light switch. Feeling something, she pushes it and the pyramid opens, as green light fills the room. Blinking her eyes a few times as they adjust to the brightness, she starts activating the doorway sequence. As the light grows in intensity, she goes over and puts her hand through one side of the platform. As she is about to pull her hand back, something on the other side grabs her and pulls her into the light. Screaming as it pulls her, she tries her best to fight whatever has her.

Waking up, Terrin thinks he hears a scream. Getting up, he wakes Tabrinia up and tells her what he thought he heard. Going into the hallway, he goes in and checks on Tanya. Looking in, he can't see her in bed. Turning the light on, he sees her bed is empty. "No", as he heads out the back door and starts towards the lab. Seeing the green light emanating from the lab, he runs over to the door, with Tabrinia on his heels.

Going down the stairs, they watch as Tanya disappears, just as they get to the bottom of the stairs. "NOOOOOOOOOOOO", Terrin yells out, as he heads for the platform.

Grabbing his arm, Tabrinia says, "Terrin..... Calm down........ We will get her back..... But you have to be in your right mind", as she continues to hold onto his arm.

Regaining his senses he says, "I'm sorry... I just got her back and now she is gone again... It's all my fault", he moans as he leans against a wall and bangs his head against it.

"Stop it, now", Tabrinia demands. "You feeling sorry for yourself and taking the blame, isn't going to help her get back".

"I know..... But we have to do something.... I can't just wait around for her to come back. I have to go and save her.... If it's the last thing I do", as he stands up, taller than ever before.

"You going in after her is not going to make any difference, until we figure out where she is".

"I know... But she is my daughter and I should be there to protect her", he replies as he starts crying for his little girl.

"We'll get her back... Don't you worry about that. First thing we need to do… Is call up Kensing and see if he is anywhere near here. That way someone can watch this doorway... Then we will go to town and pick up what you need, to finish the original doorway you created", she tells him as she holds tight to him.

"Okay... But I will never let her go, till I have her back", he replies in a dismayed tone.

"That's fine.... Just don't do anything rash like you were going to do".

"Okay... I can deal with it for now..... I just don't know how long I can hold out for, though".

"Long enough for Kensing to get here so he can at least, watch the place".

Dialing his pager number, he dials in his number and waits to see if Kensing calls back.

Sitting at a table, they are given menus and a little time to decide what they want. When the waitress comes back, he reads her nametag, which says, Arlene. "Arlene... I will start with a cup of coffee and she will have an Iced tea… Sweetened… Please".

She returns 3 minutes later with the drinks and then takes their order.

"I will have the T-bone steak, medium rare and Missy here, will have the Club sandwich".

"What kind of dressing on the salads?"

"I'll have bleu cheese and she will have Italian. Thanks", he says as she takes the menu's and leaves.

When she comes back 20 minutes later, she brings their dinners and leaves. Eating their dinner, Kensing's pager goes off, as he gets halfway through his dinner. Getting up as he looks at the number, he goes to a payphone and calls the number back. Dialing the number he waits, as it makes the connection. On the third ring, someone on the other end picks it up and says, "Hello".

"Hi. This is Kensing. Is Terrin there?"

"Hold on a sec".

"Hello Kensing. Terrin here! Where you at?"

"We're in Mobile. Why?"

"We're on our way. We will be there in about two hours".

"Okay. We will be waiting. See you shortly", Kensing replies.

"Okay. See you in a bit", Terrin replies.

Hanging the phone up, he goes to the truck and gets in. Starting the truck up, he says, "They're in Mobile at a restaurant, waiting for us. We should be there in about two hours. So if you want to sleep..... Go for it".

"Okay", as she lies down in the back seat.

Driving on towards Mobile, he tries to stay awake. Blinking his eyes every now and then, he finally is able to keep them open. Thinking about Tanya has got to get him through this whole ordeal. When he gets close to the restaurant, he gently shakes Tabrinia awake. "Tab... Time to wake up... We're almost there".

"Huh... What.... Oh... Okay, thanks", she mutters a little groggily. "We there yet?"

"Almost there.... In a few minutes we will be seeing Kensing again.... I can't wait... It's been way too long since I last seen him".

"I want to meet your best friend of so many years", Tabrinia says.

Thinking about the old days, Terrin says, "I remember one time, when we were both working and I drove up to the job site and saved his life.

He almost got knocked off the wall he was walking on. I still laugh when I think of him ducking, as I told him too", he remembers laughing.

"He sounds like a true friend", Tabrinia says.

"He is... I haven't ever known anyone else like him, or as true as he is".

"I never had any friends like that..... I wish I had".

"Well... You've got me now", Terrin replies as he smiles at her.

Smiling back she says, "I know... And I love you".

"I love you, very much too", as he smiles at her.

Pulling into a small truck stop restaurant, he says "We're here", as he parks the truck.

Getting out of the truck, they all go inside and Terrin looks around for Kensing, as a lady asks, "Can I help you?"

"Yeah.... We're looking for someone", he says as he walks into the restaurant and finally finds him.

"Sitting in the back again.....Trying to be inconspicuous?" he asks as he starts laughing.

Getting up, Kensing and Terrin hug, like the old friends they are. "Nice to see you again... Old man", Kensing says.

"Old man my ass... It's been far too long... Hasn't it?"

"Yes it has".

"Oh.... Kensing... This is Tabrinia.... My fiancé.... Tabrinia... This is my best friend..... Kensing".

"Nice to meet you" as he kisses Tabrinia's hand.

"Terrin, Tabrinia... This is my assistant... Missy".

"Hey Missy... I remember you. You lived across the street from Kensing", as a spark of recognition comes across his face.

"Hi again... Terrin... Hi Tabrinia... Nice to meet you".

"So you old dog... What the hell have you been up to? Besides being in trouble?"

"Well... Missy and I came up with a drug, that lets you use all your brain and all the ESP you can handle. The only problem is, the addiction..... We can't seem to break that barrier", he explains.

Relating to Terrin what had happened since they got taken apart from each other, Terrin relates to him all the details of what had also happened since then. Trying to fill Tabrinia in, they are all soon laughing. Leaving a few dollars for a tip, they all get up and head for the register. Paying the check, they walk outside and Terrin says, "Follow me... We should be there in about six hours. I need to stop at a shop and pick up some parts for an experiment we have been working on".

Finding an electronics shop with all the parts necessary to do what he needs to do, they head for the house. Arriving in town, they see a green glow coming from the direction of his house. As they get closer to his house, the glow gets brighter. Pulling into the drive, they see the lab doors open and the green light emanating from inside. Stopping his truck and getting out, Terrin walks over. Looking down into the lab he doesn't see much. Going down the stairs, he looks around and doesn't see anything out of place.

The pyramid is open and operating. Turning the system off, Terrin disconnects the plugs and starts searching for a reason why his system came on with no one to operate it. Not finding anything, he starts wondering if something on the other side of his doorway opened it. Or even has access to it. When Terrin went down the stairs, Tabrinia, Kensing and Missy followed him down. Looking at him, Kensing asks, "Is something wrong?"

"Yeah... The system shouldn't have been on.... We shut it down before we left.... I don't understand it.... Unless Tanya tried coming back and got it to come on", as he looks at Tabrinia.

Shrugging her shoulders she says, "You know more about it than I do".

Putting the plugs back in Terrin says, "Here's my experiment I have been working on... It's some kind of doorway, to somewhere.... I just haven't figured it out yet".

"How in the hell did you ever manage to build something like this?" Kensing asks with a strange expression on his face.

"Well... A little project taken home with added parts just seems to work when I take them back. The company loaned me some things, (of course they didn't know it)...... And a little of my money and a little bit of Tabrinia's money and here it is", Terrin states as he smiles wickedly.

"You're crazier than hell man", Kensing replies

as he starts laughing.

"Not crazy... Maybe... Ummm... Weird. But definitely not crazy", he replies as he starts laughing.

"Like I'm going to believe that".

"Believe what you want... Maybe you're the crazy one", as he starts laughing again.

"Yeah right...... Who's the one who stuck their dick in a stranger's drink? Huh?" Kensing asks as he starts laughing, remembering the incident.

"Hey... Hey... Hey... I was under the influence... I didn't have a choice", Terrin sreplies as he starts laughing himself, as he remembers the time. "It was a blast too".

"So what the hell kind of shit are you into anyway... That you are on the run?" Terrin inquires.

"Me and Missy here, were experimenting with some drugs. We kind of found a drug, that gives animals and humans, the ability to talk, using your brain. It also gives you power over others. But the drug is highly addictive. I have developed a patch and am currently using it. I kind of made the mistake of taking the first dose... And things have been different", as he thinks at Terrin, *You probably think I am crazy, but here is the proof.*

"I believe you... I see what you mean. Can you use this power and control others too?"

"Yeah... But what are you getting at?"

"Well... Tanya kind of got pulled into my doorway, by some.... Thing".

"Some..... Thing?" Kensing asks questioningly.

"Well... By the time Tabrinia and me got here... All I saw were her feet disappearing into it... After she woke us up screaming", Terrin relates as he remembers clearly what happened.

"So, what are you getting at anyway?" Kensing asks looking at him, like he knows already.

"I want you and me to go into the doorway and get Tanya and bring her back. If you don't help me..... Then I will do it myself, no matter what... But I am asking as best friends.... Will you help me on this?" Terrin pleads.

"Yeah.... I'm with you... You know that.... Damn... What kind of friend would I be if I didn't help you out, when you needed it? Besides... I may be a big asset to have along", Kensing replies as he smiles with an evilness to his grin.

"Cool... Tabrinia... Set up the frequency modulation program and run the power supply through the stand by grid deflector. Then, reverse the polarity on the micro-magnetic relays. That should put us at the same place she went too", Terrin says as he gets some special equipment ready for the trip.

"What about me? Don't I get some armor and stuff?" Kensing complains.

"I never even thought anyone else was going with me, when I got these ready. I was going to go into it myself... I just didn't know when", Terrin replies.

"That's all right. I can take care of myself... I just wanted to give you a little hell", Kensing states as he smiles at him.

"Is everyone ready?" Tabrinia asks.

Looking at each other, they nod their heads together. "Ready, anytime", Terrin says.

Powering the system up, the pyramid opens and emits the green light. Waiting for the sides to fully open Terrin looks at Kensing one last time, before he says, "See you on the other side".

"See you too", Kensing replies as he jumps into the doorway before Terrin has a chance to go.

Jumping in after him, he finds himself next to Kensing. Looking at each other, they look around and see nothing but endless red. Red clouds. Red sky. Red ground. Everything is red. "Does this place remind you of anywhere.... Like... You know.... Sort of.... Familiar?" Terrin asks Kensing.

Looking around, he nods his head, "Yeah... Like what they... You know... Say hell.... Is sort of like".

"Yeah... But where's the heat? I always thought it was supposed to be burning hot?" Terrin says puzzled.

"Yeah... I know what you mean. Well... We aren't getting anywhere like this... Come on. Let's go find your girl and get the hell out of here", Kensing says.

"Wait... Where's the door?" Terrin asks.

Looking where they came from, they don't see anything. "Oh shit.... Let’s go back the way we came and see if it is still there. If it is... We can get something and bring it from the other side and leave it at the doorway", Kensing says.

"Okay... Let's go", Terrin replies as he runs back the way he came from.

Coming out of the doorway, they see startled looks on Tabrinia's face. "What's up, Tab?" Terrin asks with a funny expression on his face.

"Nothing... I just didn't expect you back so soon", she says looking nervous.

"Okay... We were going to go look for Tanya, when we turned around and there wasn't a doorway... Or any sign of a doorway... So, we decided to come back and get something to mark the doorway, so that when we do get her, we can run through the door. Next time we come back, be ready to kill the power... Okay?" he asks.

"Yeah.... But why?"

"Because... If we can get there, they can get here", he replies with a serious look on his face.

"Okay... I'll be here waiting", she smiles at him as she watches them take the rope the dog used and jump back through the doorway.

Getting back on the other side, Terrin sets the rope down and is satisfied. Nodding his head in approval, Kensing grabs Terrin by the arm and leads him in whatever direction. "This could take some time", he says.

"I know... But... I know she's here and I want her back... No matter what", Terrin says, with a fierceness Kensing has never heard before.

"We'll get her back. Don't you worry about that", Kensing replies as he pats him on the back.

"I know... I just want to kill whatever took her", Terrin says.

"You will, unless he is already dead... If this is the place we think it is", Kensing says as he raises an eyebrow.

“Let's go and find her then", Terrin says as he starts jogging towards movement he has been noticing.

Getting closer to the movement, they see people..... Turning some kind of wheel...... But they aren't even touching the ground... How is that possible? Terrin thinks to himself. "What do you think it is?" Terrin asks.

"I don't know... Whatever it is, it's weird" Kensing replies.

Just then, floating down in the middle of the wheel, is a creature, the likes of what they have never seen before. It is about twenty feet tall. It has sort of a human appearing head, but the snout is rather long for a human. It extends out at least eighteen inches. But it has human type ears. It also has four massive horns sticking out of its head at crazy angles. One hand.... Looks like a club of some sort... And the other one looks like some kind of whip that emits small bolts, of what looks like lightning.

Ducking behind a small rock about five feet high, they watch to see what happens. As they watch, the creature starts whipping the people manning the wheel. When the whip hits the people it leaves small welts on their bodies, as they yell out in pain. Once the welts start swelling up, something comes out of them and crawls towards the creature as it rips through their skin. Once the small creatures leave the bodies, the welts no longer exist.

Using his other hand with the club, the creature hits the smaller creatures as they get near him. Squealing as they are smashed, they start coming together forming something else. Once they are all together, there is another creature......... Just like the first. Moving to the center of the wheel, as the other creature floats up, it starts beating the people with its whip. Repeating the process two more times, the last one leaves. The people are then left alone for awhile.

Walking to the left they follow the rocks around as they head in a sort of circle. As they follow it around, they find themselves in a sort of corridor. Walking down it and looking around, they see other doors that lead into other rooms that have people and creatures in them. Looking into one, a young man is being sexually assaulted by three of the creatures. Screaming out in pain as they do what they do to him, Terrin and Kensing run across the doorway in the hopes of not being seen.

Walking down the corridor they look into other rooms and see other tortures, which seem pretty outrageous. Looking into one room, Terrin whispers, "Hey... Kensing... Didn't we see this same guy in a room farther back down the hall?"

"Yeah... Wasn't he the one..... ", he starts saying, as Terrin nods his head.

Continuing on down the corridor, they come to another room. Looking in, Terrin sees the same female he saw in a previous room. "Wait a minute... Wasn't she in another room too?" Terrin whispers to Kensing.

"Hold on a sec...... Yeah, she was... Terrin... I think we're going in circles..... Let's see if we can find a way to mark where we have been", he replies as he looks around and feels in his pockets.

Finding nothing, they decide to go left then right, then right, then left, when they can so they know they are heading away from where they are. Following the corridor around, they do as they say. Looking into a room, Terrin sees the same guy as before. Instead of getting sexually assaulted though, he is being whipped by four of the creatures.

"We'll look into all the rooms as we pass them and see if they all stay the same, or if they change", Kensing says.

"Okay... Sounds good to me... I got this one", as he looks into a room and sees four females being eaten by a really big and weird creature. Once eaten, the thing starts shaking and looks like he is taking a shit. As it drops on the floor, the female he just ate rises from the stuff and gets back in line. "Ohhhh... Gross", Terrin says as he starts to wretch.

"What?" Kensing asks curiously.

"Nothing", he replies in between convulsions.

Looking into a room, Kensing sees three guys and two females and seven creatures, having an orgy. Shaking his head, he moves on to the next one. Coming right behind him, Terrin gets control of his functions and looks into another room. Looking in, he sees six of the creatures all at the wheel. It looks like their penises are all joined as one. Looking away in disgust, Terrin looks into yet another room. Seeing something far stranger than anything yet, he continues to the next one.

"If this is hell, then I sure don't want to come here", Terrin whispers to Kensing.

"I hear that", he replies looking into a room.

Looking into a room, Terrin sees Tanya, just about to be sexually assaulted by a creature. Looking up, she has tears in her eyes and is trying to say something. Grabbing Kensing's arm, Terrin says, "There she is. Let's get her", whispering to him.

"Let's go", Kensing says as they enter the room.

"Excuse me, asshole", Terrin says in as stern and strong a voice as he can muster.

Looking up, the creature lets out a roar that is almost deafening. Smiling to himself, Terrin lunges at the creature. Hitting him low, he knocks the creature off its feet. Getting up, he starts after Terrin. Getting up himself Terrin looks the creature right in the eye and says, "Hey dickface.... We aren't from here. You can't fuck with us", as he runs and kicks the creature in the chest, knocking him over again.

Getting up, the creature just looks at him. As his rage builds up, Terrin keeps his assault on the creature going until he kicks the creature. Knocking him down, the thing doesn't get back up. "Go take that to your boss.... Asshole", Terrin yells as he kicks the creature a few more times.

Going over to Tanya, Terrin releases her. "Daddy.... It’s so horrible.... Where are we?" as she hugs him tightly.

"Shhhhhh... It's all right now.... We are here to make sure you get home safely... We don't have much time, so we need to find our way out.... Are you ready to go home?" Terrin asks her.

Shaking her head, she releases him a little, but still hugs him. Going back the way they came, they look into some of the rooms and look at each other as if saying something privately. Going down the corridor, they stop as they see four creatures come out from a room ahead. Seeing them, the creatures start making weird noises. Looking behind them, Terrin sees six more coming from behind them. "Oh shit..... We have company behind us too", Terrin tells him.

Looking behind them Kensing sees the other ones. "Damn.... I think we just bought a front row ticket to hell", Kensing says as he tries to control some of them.

"Well.... At least they can only come at us one at a time...", Terrin starts saying as the hallway starts widening, letting all the creatures take up the hallway.

"Now we're in trouble", Kensing replies as he makes one fight another one with his mind control.

Reaching in his pocket, Kensing finds two more patches and slaps them on. Feeling the rush he can also feel the strength he now has. Controlling three of the creatures, he gets the six on one side fighting each other. Turning towards the others, he tries to control the other ones and he gets them fighting amongst themselves. Just then from above, comes this creature that is at least forty-five feet tall.

With a head that is so grotesque, it is hard to even explain. But the horns! There are two horns sticking out of its head and two sticking out of the elbows. The eyes burn bright red. The body is that of many different kinds of things. Some so hideous that there are no words to explain them. In other words, it would take many pages to really explain what it truly looks like. Just believe me when I say, it is hideously grotesque. Anyway, as we were telling you, it came down from above and alit about fifty feet in front of us.

Looking at us, it starts to speak in a tongue we couldn't even guess at. Shaking our heads to see if he understood no, Terrin said, "Hey asshole...... We came here to get my daughter, who was stolen from me..... We got her and now we are leaving...... ".

"And don't try to stop us", Kensing says in a very challenging voice, as his eyes blaze redder than even the creatures.

Stepping back a few feet, the creature finally speaks to us, through telepathy. *What is it you want here?*

We only came here to get his daughter, whom was kidnapped by your minions.

Fools. You think you can come here and just leave? What do I look like..... A fool?

If you want to know what you look like, maybe you should get a mirror.... Oops... Sorry. You would probably break it.

How dare, you speak to me that way. You will now pay the price for trespassing in my home. You will never leave here and you will never get back to where you are going. As we speak, my so-called minions are crossing over to your world. HAhahahahahaaaaa, it roars with laughter in their heads.

Feeling like his head is going to explode from the thing's laughing in his head, Terrin says, "Hey... Asshole.... Who in the hell made you a god?"

I made myself... Fool. How dare you challenge me... I will win as I always do.

"Eat me asshole. You will never win, cause you are too damn weak. Sheeesh... What a moronic idiot".

You will pay for that remark. You will suffer here, for eternity.

"I think maybe you got that wrong. You better pray to all the demons you can, cause we are here to kick your miserable ass back to the deepest pits you crawled out of", Terrin states standing his ground firmly.

Blowing steam from it's face, it's eyes get redder than red. They are blood red. He roars, as he is about to charge. Coming at them Terrin says, "Kensing... You better do something and quick".

"Why.... You're the one that pissed it off. You take him", Kensing says as he starts to walk away.

"Kensing.... NOW's not the time to be fucking with me", Terrin says with a serious look on his face.

"Okay... But then you owe me", he says. "Deal?" "Deal", Terrin says as they shake hands.

Turning toward the thing, Kensing concentrates harder than he has ever had to before. Thinking of the thing hitting an invisible wall, the thing stops instantly, as pus-like stuff starts spewing out of its face. Roaring out in anger at being stopped, the thing still tries to go forward. Not getting anywhere, it tries to break in on Kensing's thoughts.

CHAPTER 5

When the guys crossed over the second time, Missy started saying things like, "Where am I? How did I get here? Who are you?"

"Relax Missy. I am Tabrinia. Don't you remember?" she asks wonderingly.

"No... The last thing I remember, is Kensing and me getting a truck so he could go north to meet his friend. Other than that, I don't remember", she says with a puzzled look on her face.

"Well, you are now up north with him. I 'm Terrin's fiancé. Kensing's best friend is Terrin, isn't it?" Tabrinia asks.

"Yeah.... Okay... So we are with his best friend and where is he at?"

"He's in the doorway. They went in after Terrin's daughter, who was snatched into the doorway by some...thing", Tabrinia explains.

"Okay... I can deal with it a little better... So... When he crosses the doorway, his power quits. Okay... I will fix him", she says as she goes upstairs.

"Missy. Where are you going?"

"I'm going to take the drug that makes Kensing able to control people with his mind", she states.

"Wait.... I can't leave in case they come back", Tabrinia says trying to get her to stay.

Not listening, Missy goes up the stairs and out to the truck. Opening the back up, she finds the case with the patches in them. Taking one out of the package, she slaps it on her arm. As the drug starts to take effect of her body, she starts having these really bad cramps. Bending over, they only get worse. Trying to rip the patch off, she finally does but only after the drug has made her an addict.

Gagging as the drug keeps working on her, she falls to the floor. Screaming out in pain, she finally feels a relief go through her body as she gets back to normal. Able to finally stand up, she gets up and takes a patch just in case. Pocketing it she goes back downstairs to the lab. As she gets to the bottom step, she sees this most horrid creature coming out of the doorway. Screaming as she sees it coming after her, she turns and runs back up the stairs.

When Tabrinia saw the creature come out, she instantly shut the power off to the system. When she powered the system down, she saw the rope drop to the ground. So... Whatever gets caught in the doorway, when it is powered down will get cut off she thinks to herself. Looking around she sees if there is anything she can use as a weapon. Not seeing anything she runs for the stairs. Grabbing her hair, the creature pulls her back.

As she ran down the stairs, Missy had some weird thoughts. Running anywhere, but where the creature is she stops and thinks to herself... Wait a minute. What am I so scared for. I will just put a full strength patch on. Taking the patch out of her pocket, she slaps it on her arm. Sitting down as she waits for the cramps to start, she feels a sudden rush go through her entire body. Shaking her head, she tries to clear the thoughts that come pouring in. None of them good either. Running up the stairs, she trips. Getting herself up off the ground, she goes to the truck and gets a couple of more patches. Putting another one on she feels the rush even stronger this time.

Breathing in deeply, it feels like she is breathing in the cleanest air ever. Going back to the stairs, she goes down as she looks for the creature. When she is almost all the way down, something grabs her foot. As she starts to fall she thinks, I wish I could fly right now so I wouldn't fall down and feel the pain. Just as that thought crossed her mind, she started floating down. Stopping altogether she floats back up and turns around. Looking the creature in the eyes she says, "You better give me my friend, or there will be hell to pay", as her eyes glow a dark red and her smile is the wickedest Tabrinia has ever seen.

Bringing Tabrinia out from behind the stairs, Missy then tells her to power up the doorway. "We are going to send him back to where he came from", as she keeps her gaze riveted on the creature.

Powering the system up, she activates the

control for the doorway. The pyramid starts to open. When the sides are about halfway down, they stop. "Oh shit", Tabrinia says as she looks for the problem.

Looking around for anything that might have come unplugged, she finds nothing. Trying to close the pyramid, it still doesn't budge. Getting irate as she tries to locate the problem, she goes next to the pyramid and looks all around it.

"What's wrong?" Missy asks.

"The pyramid won't open all the way. I can't figure it out", Tabrinia replies as she looks around.

"Stay", Missy says to the creature. "What about this?" she asks as she shows her a plug that is not plugged in.

"No... That's a spare hookup for the control panel. It has to be something internal and I don't know enough about it to take it apart and fix it", Tabrinia explains.

Looking over at the creature, Missy sees it is gone. "Oh damn. It's gone", Missy says as she heads for the stairs and looks for the creature.

"Wait....", Tabrinia starts out to say, as she sees it is falling on deaf ears.

Going outside and looking for the creature, Missy looks everywhere. Looking intently at the ground, she looks for footprints even. Finding nothing she closes her eyes and concentrates on any odd thoughts. Sensing nothing near she looks around the house. Going around the house first one way, then the other, she can't seem to find it anywhere near the house. Following her instincts, she starts off in the direction it may have gone.

When Missy left the lab, Tabrinia kept looking for a way to get the doorway open. Using her amprobe, she sees everything that is supposed to get power is receiving power. Not finding anything wrong with the pyramid she gets frustrated and just hauls off and kicks it, as she says, "Stupid piece of shit".

Just then the pyramid started opening again. Jumping back as it opens up, she is startled until she starts laughing as she realizes that it just needed a good, swift, kick in the ass. "I can't believe I am so stupid", she says out loud but not realizing it, until Missy comes back down the stairs and says, "Talking to any one in particular...... Wall?" as she starts laughing.

"No.... Just trying to get some intelligent answers", she says as she starts laughing along with her.

"Then you better talk to me then", as she laughs louder.

As they get control of themselves, Tabrinia asks, "Can you handle anything if they get through?"

"Yeah"... As she slaps another patch on...."Ohhhhhhh"....... As the rush goes through her entire body making it tingle...... "Do it", she says as the rush fades slightly.

"Setting power levels and fluctuational micro-magnetic values", as she engages the systems total power, the doorway turns bright green.

"I'm pushing them back", Missy says as she laughs slightly.

"It's open all the way. I hope it's in the same

place. Here... Help me toss this rope in", Tabrinia says.

Going over to her, they throw the rope into the doorway. Once the rope is through, something pulls on it pulling them down. Getting back up, they tie the rope off to a rod sticking out of the ground. "Hey Missy... I think you need to go through and see if the other rope is still there", Tabrinia says.

"I don't know about that", she hedges.

"You are the only one that can fend these things off".

"Yeah... But these are strange and ugly things... What if I screw up?"

"Don't worry... It'll be all right. I have faith in you", Tabrinia says as she tries to encourage her.

"Okay... But if something goes wrong... Then I don't want to be held responsible... Okay?"

"Okay... I won't blame you for anything. I just need to find out if the doorway appears in the same spot".

"Okay... Here I go", Missy yells as she jumps into the doorway.

Appearing on the other side, she sees about fifteen of the same creatures that got away. Looking around for the other rope, she only sees the rope they just tossed through. Fending off the creatures as she tries to locate the rope, she gives up and goes back through the doorway. Coming through where she left she says as she comes out, "No... I didn't see any rope except the one we just threw into the doorway", she reports back. "There are also a bunch of those creatures, waiting on the other side though".

"You keep them back. I have a feeling the doorway doesn't always appear in the same place. So that means, they have to locate where it's at, before they can get back", she says as she thinks and wonders, if maybe she isn't putting something in wrong.

Checking all the figures to the ones he told her to put in, she sees they are exactly the same. Shaking her head, she can't figure where the problem is then. It must be some kind of random doorway, she thinks. "Hey Missy. I wonder what would happen if we shut the system down and restarted it. If there would be a way... To at least... Locate the door somewhere near where it was, when they went in", she asks wonderingly.

"I guess it can't hurt to try. Let me pull the rope back through, if I can", she replies as she grabs the rope and starts pulling it.

Coming freely through the doorway, it stops after a short time. Jerking on it, she pulls with all her might and a creature started coming through the doorway. As it got about halfway through, Tabrinia cut all power and cut the creature in half. Squealing as she shut the doorway down, the top half of the creature jerks around. Watching it they are both transfixed by the way it just keeps flopping, like a fish out of water. As they watch it, they suddenly find it amusing and they both start laughing as they watch it flopping around.

"That is the funniest thing I have seen in a long time", Missy says as she continues

laughing.

"It's been awhile for me too", Tabrinia replies.

Seeing a fire extinguisher hanging on the wall, Missy grabs it and takes it over by the creature. Standing over it she raises the cylinder and smacks the creature four times before it quits moving. "Quick... Open the doorway", Missy says as she gets ready to throw it back into the doorway.

Reactivating the system, she opens the doorway. "Go in also and see if you see the rope, from the first time", Tabrinia says as she puts the exact figures into the computer. "Here it goes", as it turns bright green.

Trying to pick up the remains of the creature, Missy just can't seem to get it. Coming over to her, Tabrinia helps her toss the thing into the doorway. Stepping through herself Missy looks around and sees what is there. No rope anywhere. Just a few creatures coming towards her. Going back through, she tells Tabrinia to shut it down and try again. Wrong place. Shutting the system down and reactivating it yet again, she watches as Missy goes through.

Once through Missy sees what seems to be a wheel, up ahead, with people pushing it. Looking around everywhere else she sees something off in the distance. Whether it's a rope, or not, is hard to tell. Going toward it she feels something strange in her mind. Pushing out with all her might, she feels the creatures coming for her. Running towards the thing she saw, she sees it is the rope so she starts back to the doorway.

About halfway back, she stops as three of the

creatures approach her from the wheel. Breathing smoke out their nostrils they fume and send out telepathy impulses. Pulling a patch from her pocket, Missy slaps it on. Feeling the rush of the drug, she looks at the creatures and thinks of a wall that pushes them backward. Just then they are stopped in their tracks. They are then being pushed back, as she walks forward.

Smiling and nodding, she gets to the doorway and stands guard. Sending out a signal to Kensing, she tries to tell him she is here and waiting. Not knowing whether he got the message or not, she tries a few more times. After waiting for what seems like a half an hour, she goes back through the doorway. "Nothing. I can't seem to get any kind of response", she tells Tabrinia as she comes through the doorway.

"Something happened. It had to have. Maybe we should go after them?" Tabrinia says.

"No. If anything I will just go through the doorway every now and then. That way, I can monitor the progress of the creatures too", Missy replies. "If you can go up to the truck and get me the case marked caution: special patches it would help a great deal", she adds.

"Okay. Just be careful", Tabrinia says as she goes up the stairs and to the truck.

Waiting for Tabrinia to get back, Missy feels uneasy about this. Something just seems off. Not paying any attention to the voice she shrugs it off. Getting over her uneasy feeling, Tabrinia comes down the stairs and asks, "This case?"

"Perfect", Missy smiles as she takes the case and opens it. Taking about five of the patches out of the case, she says, "I'm off to see the fuckin' wizard", she says as she laughs wickedly, while jumping into the doorway.

Watching her go through, Tabrinia feels like something isn't right. Shrugging it off, she just hopes she can control the creatures long enough to get the guys back. When she went through the doorway, she felt this odd sensation. Shrugging it off she starts sending out her pulses. Walking towards the people pushing the wheel, she sees the same thing Terrin and Kensing saw. The creature coming down and whipping them. Then the welts coming out their backs and crawling towards the creature. He then smashed the creatures and they then grew into another creature.

Shaking her head in disbelief, she moves around to the left of the wheel. Looking for anything that might lead her to them, she continues to walk on.

CHAPTER 6

Laughing as the creature smacked into the barrier, they head back the way they were going and where they guess they came from. Making the creatures fight each other, they make it past without a hitch. Trying to remember which way they came, Terrin makes a few wild guesses, as he is not sure. Looking into rooms as they pass them, they look familiar but then most of the rooms had the same people in them.

Not knowing where they are Terrin says, "I think were lost... Man".

"What makes you think that?" Kensing asks him with a snicker on his face.

"Well, for one thing... I remember looking into a lot of the rooms and seeing the same people, but doing different things though".

"I know. I looked to. I saw the same things you saw. At this point it's just hit or miss. If we miss, we go back and start another way", Kensing replies sarcastically.

"Oh, Fuck you asshole", Terrin replies as he smiles.

"That's Mr. Asshole to you", Kensing responds as he starts cracking up laughing.

While they are cracking on each other and laughing four creatures try to sneak up on them. Sensing them long before they get too close, Kensing erects a barrier that halts them about twenty- five feet away. Smiling secretly to himself, he leads them away so they won't know. Turning right at the next intersection, they continue looking into rooms. Trying to keep Tanya from looking in, she gets glances every now and then anyway. Covering her mouth at times, she tries not to look but can't seem to help it.

Getting grossed out at times himself, he looks away as soon as he sees something that revolts him. As Terrin looks into this one room he sees something he hasn't seen before. "Hey.... Kensing... This is the wrong way".

"How do you know?" he asks with a sarcastic tone to his voice.

"Because.... I have seen a room we haven't seen before. That's how", he replies as he smiles.

"Ohhhh.... And that makes you an expert on the subject?" Kensing asks sneeringly.

"That's right... I am more than just a brain.... I'm a body too", Terrin says as he starts laughing.

"Yeah... Real funny asshole", Kensing replies as he starts laughing with him.

Continuing down the way they were going, they find other things that just don't seem to fit. Not in this place anyway. I mean.... What is a dude with wings, doing down here? Terrin wonders. Or what about the other dude, who is encased in a bright light? Shrugging it off he is just amazed and awed by all the people and other creatures here. Following the rest of the group he keeps looking into the rooms. Shaking his head at times, he looks up and sees the big badass dude coming for them.

"Kensing.... Look", Terrin says as he points.

Looking at what he is pointing to he sees the big dude too. "Don't worry. I will take care of this asshole", as he starts concentrating with his mind.

Staring at it with everything he has, he is thinking of a big club coming down on top of its head. Just then, a hammer that is about four feet in diameter, comes down and smashes on top of its head. Screaming out in rage it starts coming faster. Terrin and Tanya run back the way they came, as Kensing does what he can. "Be careful", Terrin says as they take off.

Looking over his shoulder at them Kensing sees they are leaving. "Hey.... Wait for me", he says as he runs after them.

Letting the thing get as close as he dares, he finally turns and blasts it with a pure energy beam. Hitting it square in the chest it rips right through the thing leaving a hole big enough for an average man to walk through. Turning around he follows after them again, as the thing stands there stunned. Screaming a cry of rage so loud it hurts their ears, it continues on its rampage after them.

As they run blindly ahead, looking over their

shoulders every now and then Terrin and Tanya run right into six of the creatures. Getting hold of them they start hauling them into a room. "Kensing.......... Heeeeeeelp", Terrin yells out as they get them.

Hearing Terrin's yell Kensing turns a corner and doesn't see anything or anyone down the corridor. "TERRIN..... TANYA", he yells out.

"Down here", he hears faintly.

Trying to follow the voice he runs down the corridor. Looking into rooms every now and then he looks into one and sees Terrin getting beaten. Shaking his head he pushes the creature away. Looking up Terrin smiles as he gets up. Standing up he runs at the creature and kicks it squarely in the chest, knocking it on its ass. Growling fiercely, it gets back up and starts towards Terrin. "Behind you", Kensing says.

Turning around he is knocked down as the creature plows into him. Falling down, his breath gets knocked out of him. Catching his breath as the creature stands over him he brings his foot straight up and into the crotch, hoping it can be hurt. Laughing in an inhuman way it reaches down and picks Terrin up by the throat. Kicking the thing in its chest, it drops him as it grabs it chest.

Hitting the ground, Terrin stands up and kicks the thing again. Knocking it to the ground he goes over and starts kicking it repeatedly as he screams obscenities at it. Laughing as Terrin goes to town on the creature, Kensing is soon on the floor grabbing his gut. "And what the hell do you think you are laughing at?" Terrin asks

Kensing.

"Yo.... O...... U", as he continues to laugh. "You man. I haven't ever seen anything... Like that before", he says as he starts laughing again.

"Fuck you asshole. I was pissed cause of what he was going to do to me", he explains.

"That's all right. I can use a good laugh every now and then", Kensing replies.

"Which reminds me. We need to find Tanya again. They took her down this way", he says as he leads him out into the corridor.

Running down the way he saw them taking her, they start looking into rooms as they pass them. Not seeing any sign of her, they continue the way they were going. Turning corners at random they look for what seems like hours when Terrin finally finds her, in a room surrounded by eight of the things. Whispering to Kensing, Terrin asks, "Hey... Can you hold them while I get her?"

Nodding his head he starts concentrating on them. Pointing his finger he shakes his finger and nods his head, telling him to go. Running into the room, Terrin grabs Tanya up and takes her out of there as they watch. Not being able to do anything they just watch. Heading the way they were coming from, they roam just looking for the way they came in. Not having any luck, Terrin looks at his watch and sees they have been here for at least thirteen hours.

Shaking his head as they look for the way out, he looks into other rooms to see if they might be able to get out that way. Not seeing anything, except the same people getting beat, maimed and sexually abused. "Kensing... Let's start making right hand and then two left turns and see where that takes us", Terrin suggests shrugging his shoulders.

"Okay... Sounds as good as anything else. Starting now", Kensing replies.

Putting Tanya down she finally wakes up and smiles as she sees her Dad's face. "What happened?" she asks as if disoriented.

"Never mind. We will tell you all about it when we finally get out of this hellhole", Terrin tells her as Kensing and him start laughing.

"What's so funny?' she asks questioningly.

"Nothing. Just a private joke between Kensing and me. Nothing you should worry about", Terrin replies.

"C'mon...... Let's go", Kensing tells them trying to hurry them up.

"Were coming.... Don't be so damned impatient", Terrin says as he asks Tanya if she is able to walk on her own.

Shaking her head she stands up and starts walking with them. Turning right they go left at the next intersection. Not seeing anything they go left once more. Looking in rooms as they go they still can't tell where they are. Walking around, Terrin says, "Anyone else hungry besides me?"

"Yeah.... I'm starving", Tanya says.

"I've been hungry... Just didn't want to say anything", Kensing replies.

"I wonder if they have anything we could... You know... Eat around here", Terrin wonders out loud.

"First order of business. Find food and water", Kensing says.

Walking down the corridor they all start looking into the rooms, as they pass them. Not finding anything, they all hope to get out of here before they starve to death. Watching out for anything that even, remotely looks edible, they continue on their trip. "Hey, Terrin...... Didn't you say you wanted to take over hell when you got there? NOW's your chance", Kensing says as he starts laughing.

"I don't think so.... I meant after I died. You are such an asshole.... I swear", Terrin replies sarcastically.

"You two are as crazy as everyone says you are", Tanya adds to their conversation.

"Oh damn.... She speaks", Kensing says as him and Terrin both start cracking up laughing.

"Shut up", Tanya whines as only kids can.

"Baby... Baby.... Baby", Kensing says as they keep laughing.

"Stop it", Tanya demands.

"I'm sorry", Terrin says as he tries to look sad, but can only look at her and start smirking.

"Dad... You aren't supposed to make fun of me", she whines even louder.

"I'm sorry", he says as he looks her in the eyes and means it, this time.

Hugging him they continue their search, for either the doorway or something to at least eat. Looking into one room he passes, Terrin sees what looks like apples or something like it in a small basket in the room. "Hey guys... Check this out and tell me what you think".

Going over to the door Kensing looks in and says, "Looks like food to me".

"Me too", as Tanya peeks as well.

Going into the room, they go over to the basket and Terrin pokes one of the objects with his finger. Feeling that it has substance, he picks one up and starts to squeeze it lightly. It's firm, yet gives slightly. Trying to break a piece off, he finally squishes it. As it squishes it makes a hell of a mess. Dripping a red, pulpy mass all over, Terrin throws it down. "Yech", he exclaims.

"What in the hell is that?" Kensing asks as if Terrin should know.

"How am I supposed to know?" Terrin asks back.

"You're the one who made the doorway. I just figured you've already been places", Kensing states as if he has all the facts readily available.

"I just got it done. I was just going to go in, when I had to get out of there. This is the first time anyone has ever been through it", he explains.

"Ohhhhhhh..... I see.... You have only been making it not going into it. So..... What were you looking for... A lab rat?" Kensing asks as he looks at Terrin and smiles.

"Right", Terrin replies as he smiles back at him. "Does anyone want to try it?", he asks as he holds a new piece of apple out.

Shaking their heads, he throws it down and they leave. Going back to the routine of walking and looking, they know they are lost. Turning left they find themselves heading down a different corridor. This one actually has ceilings in it. "This could be it", Kensing exclaims excitedly.

"I hope so", Terrin says. "I am about tired of this damned place".

"I think we all are", Kensing says.

"I know I am", Tanya replies.

Heading down the corridor they keep looking into the rooms. Seeing what looks familiar, Terrin shrugs his shoulders thinking it's probably my imagination. When they are about twenty-five feet down the corridor, they hear a loud roar coming from behind them. As they all turn around, they see the big dude coming at them faster than they ever thought possible. "HOLY SHIT", Terrin screams out as he grabs Tanya's arm and leads her down the corridor.

Looking back Kensing sees them running down the corridor leaving him behind. Nodding his head, he didn't expect any different. He has all the power. Trying to create a barrier, the creature keeps coming at him. "FUCK YOU", he shouts as he turns and runs after the other two.

Looking ahead as they run, Terrin sees a dead-end coming up and no other corridors to go down. "Ohh shit", Terrin says as he turns around and sees Kensing coming after him. "Dead-end", Terrin exclaims.

Catching up with them he sees the dead-end as Terrin says it. Turning around they see the big bastard coming down the corridor. Backing up as the creature gets closer, they wonder why they haven't hit the wall yet. Turning around Terrin takes a quick look. Turning his head back and forth, he can't believe what happened. "Kensing... We are in the wall. I think it was an illusion, so we couldn't find our way out", he says.

"No wonder we couldn't find it", Kensing replies.

Looking back, he can't see the creature's anymore, all he sees is just a wall. Turning around, they see the rope lying on the ground not more than twenty feet away.

CHAPTER 7

Coming back through the doorway, Missy says she can't seem to find them anywhere. She then tells her what she saw. Shaking her head in disbelief, Tabrinia says, "You're kidding.... Right?"

"No, I'm not", Missy replies as she looks dead serious.

"I want to see. This is hard to comprehend", Tabrinia says.

"Is it safe to leave without anyone here?"

"Yeah... Sure", Tabrinia says.

"Okay...... Let's go", Missy says as she steps through the doorway.

Following Missy, Tabrinia goes through the doorway and is totally amazed at what she sees. "Oh my god", she says as she looks at everything.

"C'mon..... Look at this", Missy says as she tries to get her to come over and see the wheel for herself.

Going over to her, she looks and sees exactly what Missy described to her to a tee. "You were right", Tabrinia says. "But, I think we should get back now".

"Okay. Let's go", Missy says as they head for the doorway.

Getting to where the rope is, they jump towards it when they are a couple of feet away. Landing on the other side of the rope, they are stunned. "What the hell happened to the doorway?" Tabrinia asks.

"You got me. I think we are in trouble now. What do you think happened?" she asks Tabrinia.

"I don't know. But if the guys come back and find us here, but there's no doorway.... Oooooooohhh, are they gonna be pissed", she replies.

"There's nothing we can do about it now. If they find us and there's no doorway, they can only be so pissed. We didn't know this was going to happen", Missy says.

"I know. But there is nothing we can do. I can't even think of what went wrong", Tabrinia says with a serious look on her face.

"There are only so many possibilities. But it doesn't do us any good. We need to see what we can do though..... I can't imagine what happened", she says as she starts to break down.

"Missy.... Calm down..... We will figure something out..... I hope", as she tries to console her.

Sobbing like a baby as she realizes what this could mean, Missy cries her heart out to Tabrinia. When she finally gets her emotions under control, they start walking and looking for a place to hide. Finally coming up on a place they rest, as they keep an alert eye out for any creatures. After a short time, Tabrinia says, "We need to do something.... I can't just sit here and not do anything. Do you have any of those patches with you?" she asks Missy.

"Uhhh... Yeah... Here", she says as she pulls a couple out of her pocket and hands them to her.

Taking the patches, she peels one off and slaps it on her arm. All of a sudden she starts getting cramping pains in her stomach. Bending over as they get worse, she falls to the ground as she grabs at her stomach. Her body finally goes into convulsions as the drug takes full effect of her. The pain subsides, as she rises and shakes her head. "Wow!", she exclaims as she feels the drugs mental abilities. "This is so cool.... If I had known this sooner, I may have taken it then", she says.

"Yeah... But now you have to take it for the rest of your life. What is Terrin going to say, when he sees you are hooked on this drug?" she asks.

"I'll say, I couldn't help it. Circumstances forced me to take it..... You know.... Things happened... And before I knew it.... I was on the drug", as she smiles raising an eyebrow.

Laughing as Tabrinia says that, Missy says, "He may buy it... But if he doesn't... Here is what you can say", as she whispers in her ear and they both burst out laughing.

Just then a creature appears from around the

edge of the rocks, (if that is what you call them), and roars as it sees them talking and laughing. Looking up as the creature roars, they both use their mental powers and force the creature back. Peeling the other patch Tabrinia slaps it on and falters for a few seconds as the drug kicks in. Pushing with even more power now, she forces the creature back even faster.

Smiling as the creature keeps going back, she sees the edge of a cliff coming up behind the creature. Walking a little faster and feeling more confident of herself she gives one final push and flings the creature over the edge. Roaring as it falls, it alerts more creatures. Turning around Missy says, "Ummmmm... Tab... We have... Ummmmm..... Company", she says as calmly as she can.

Turning around Tabrinia sees about twenty of the creatures, coming for them. Going into action Tabrinia thinks for a minute and smiles as she concentrates real hard. Feeling herself getting lighter, she looks down and sees she is floating a couple of inches off the ground. Grabbing Missy's arm, she jumps off the edge as she says, "Trust me..... Concentrate real hard on floating.... And it will happen", she tries to explain.

As they both concentrate real hard, they feel themselves floating. Opening her eyes and looking down, Tabrinia smiles as she sees they are a couple of hundred feet from the bottom. Looking around, she sees another ledge just below them. "Keep concentrating and open your eyes", she says.

Opening her eyes, she looks ahead and sees the ledge just below them, but about eighty feet away. "Okay... Now what?" she asks back.

"Let's see if we can make it to that ledge... If so, we can rest for a little bit and then go looking for.... Whatever.... I don't know. At least we will be alive and free for now", she says as she smiles lightly.

"What good does that do us now?" she asks back with a questioning look on her face.

"I don't know", she replies as she thinks about the ledge.

Floating towards the ledge, they arrive and rest for a few minutes. "What's next?" Missy asks.

"I guess just keep going until we find whatever it is we need, to get the hell out of here", she says not realizing exactly where they are at.

"Whatever... I just don't want to be stuck here..... Forever", Missy says looking down.

"Don't worry.... Things will work out. Have a little faith in yourself", Tabrinia tells her as she tries to give her a little self-confidence.

Smiling she says, "Okay.... We will make it", then she asks, "Won't we?"

"Yes we will. Calm down and don't worry so damn much", Tabrinia says as she gets up.

Getting up and onto her feet also they start heading down the tunnel. Not being able to see too hot, there is a red glow everywhere but it gets hard to see anything, like a junction or something where they can turn. By the time they finally do see one, they are already in it and exposed for all to see, whoever happens to be coming the other way. "I don't like this", Missy says.

"I don't either... But you don't hear me complaining... Do you?" she asks rather sarcastically.

"Ohhh.... Just go to hell", she retorts back.

"I'm getting the feeling I am already there", she replies as she smiles slightly and then gets a sour look on her face.

"What?" Missy asks.

"Nothing... Just remembering something", Tabrinia says.

As they walk on, they look for anything edible as they start to get hungry. Looking anywhere they might find something, they find nothing but empty rooms. Shaking their heads they continue on. Walking as if they are a couple of zombies, they search but without any luck.

CHAPTER 8

Seeing the rope, they head for it. Running for the rope, they expect to be back in the lab when they get to it. Running they get to the rope and keep going. Looking up and seeing the same landscape as they have been in, Terrin says. "What the hell happened to the doorway?"

"You got me buddy. Maybe they had to close it down. Maybe the creatures started coming across. Who knows", Kensing says as he shrugs his shoulders.

"Not me... That's for sure", he replies sarcastically.

Looking to his left, Kensing sees a crowd of the creatures. Watching them, they see the creatures looking down at something and roaring loudly. When the creatures turn around they see them and start coming towards them. "Hey.... Terrin.... We have some.... Like.... Company", Kensing states as he taps him on the shoulder.

Looking where Kensing is looking, Terrin sees all the creatures heading for them. "Ohhh shit", he says.

Looking around, Kensing and Terrin look for

anything that might help them out. Not seeing anything substantial, they start running. "Dad... I'm tired... I want to go home", Tanya whines.

"Don't we all dear. I can't do anything about it right now. First we need to find somewhere we can hide out at. At least until we can get rid of these creatures", Terrin replies as he tries to smile.

Running as if their lives depended on it, (actually it does), they don't find anything except the room with the wheel and the maze. "Let's go back into the maze", Kensing says as he heads for where he thinks it is.

Following him they see him disappear up ahead of them. Running into the wall they find themselves, back in the damned maze. "I hate this fuckin' place", Terrin says as he shakes his head.

"Daddy... Watch your language", Tanya reminds him.

"Oops.... Sorry", he says as he looks at her with a sad look.

Smiling at him she said, "That's all right. I forgive you this time".

"Okay. Thanks", he replies back, as he smiles.

Going through the maze, they go in a certain pattern so they can easily find their way back. Looking in the rooms like usual, they see the same thing they had seen already. Looking into one, Terrin sees a nice looking babe, she's doing something to one of the creatures. Staring a little longer, he finally realizes what it is she is doing. Shaking his head and trying not to wretch, he looks away and follows after them.

Looking back as he catches up, Terrin sees the big guy coming after them again. "Kensing... Run like hell is on your feet. Here comes the big dude again", he says as he runs a little faster.

Looking back he sees what Terrin is talking about. Coming to a stop he concentrates real hard on a wall that will stop the thing. Smashing into it, the thing roars out a defeatful cry. Turning around and running again he finally catches up with the other two. "C'mon. Hurry it up", he says turning a corner.

Running for their lives, they run right into the lab. Running into the control panel Terrin flips over it, as he hits it. "Hey... What the hell happened?" he asks, as he starts to get up.

"I guess the doorway was in the maze", Kensing replies.

"Shutting system down...... Shut down initiated", Terrin says as the system shuts down. "So where the hell are the girls?" he asks as he shakes his head.

"I don't know", Kensing replies giving him an 'I don't know look.'

"Quick.... Upstairs and see if they are in the house", Terrin says as he runs up the stairs.

Following after him, they search the house, but can't find anyone. Going back to the lab, Terrin muses, "I wonder if they went into the doorway.... And maybe… It somehow got shut down..... And the power went off while they were in and they got stuck in there".

"Could have. Which means we need to find them before we can do anything else", Kensing replies looking at the floor.

"I'm not sure what the deal is, but I think, maybe the doorway doesn't always appear in the same place. It may change its location, in which case, we need to power the system up and down until we can locate them. Okay. I will initiate power up sequence.... Then you can go through once the doorway is open and look around for them. At each location, we will spend one hour there and then return", Terrin says as he powers the system up.

"Sounds good to me", Kensing replies. "Anytime you 're ready.... I am".

"Okay.... It's open", he says as the sides hit the floor and the green light comes from the pyramid.

Jumping through, Kensing looks around and sees if he sees anything familiar. Not recognizing anything, he walks around and gets his bearings for the doorway. Not finding them at this place, he goes back into the lab and reports, no luck. Powering down the system and then up again, Terrin says, "It's ready".

Jumping through again, he comes face to face with one of the creatures, but a smaller version. Shaking his head, he imagines a wall between him and the creature. The creature reaches up and is about to strangle him, when it hits an invisible barrier. Laughing as he steps back through the doorway and into the lab, he just misses the girls. Reporting that they are not there, they try another time.

Trying for hours, but having no success, they send Tanya up to the house, for food and drinks, while they continue on. Plugging away at the doorway, they go from location to location and sometimes find a location that is the same as one he went through before. Going through one doorway, he finds himself in a maze, but this one has ceilings in it. Looking around, he turns a corner and walks down the corridor for a short time.

When he turned the corner, he missed seeing the girls again. They went down the corridor he had just come from. When they passed the junction, they walked right around the corner and missed the doorway, by about four feet. Had they walked straight ahead, they would have been back in the lab.

Walking back to the doorway, Kensing goes in and tells him that they aren't there as far as he can tell. When he came back, Tanya had sandwiches and drinks for all of them. Eating while they take a break, they begin their routine again. Powering up, then down, when they don't find them and then back up again. Tediousness in a rather exciting time.

CHAPTER 9

Walking endlessly, they can't seem to find anything they can use or eat. Looking into rooms, they see some pretty sick things that the creatures are doing to the humans involved. "Hey Tabrinia.... What say we take a break in the next empty room for a bit…? I am dog-dead tired?" Missy asks.

"Okay... So lets find one then", she replies as they walk on and keep looking.

Finding an empty room was a little tougher than they ever thought it would be. It seemed that every room they looked into through a doorway had someone occupying it at the time. Finally, after what seems like hours, they find one and go in. Taking turns sleeping, the other keeps watch. Not having any company while Missy slept, Tabrinia wakes her up and then goes to sleep herself.

Dreaming of having a happy and fulfilling relationship with Terrin, she smiles as she sleeps. All of a sudden, her dream turned into a nightmare. Her and Terrin were making love, when all of a sudden, she opened her eyes and saw it was one of the creatures she was in bed with. Screaming at the top of her voice, she is rudely awakened as Missy tries to hold off the creatures coming in the door.

Waking up, she sees the creatures and helps Missy push them out the door. Finally getting them out the door, she is wide-awake as they look into the corridor and see the creatures walking down it. Heading out the door away from the creatures, they begin looking for anything that might come in handy.

Walking down a corridor, they turn right at the next junction and just miss seeing Kensing. Walking along for awhile, they are soon so hungry, they are beginning to get irritable and cranky from no food. As they walk Tabrinia says, "I want the hell out of here".

"It's all your fault", Missy says snidely.

"I knew it... I knew you were going to say that. What makes it my fault?" she asks.

"You were the one who left the controls. If you hadn't of ever came in, we wouldn't be in this predicament", she blurts out.

"That's so much bullshit. You think I had something to do with this, huh?" she asks in as rough a voice as she can muster up.

"You probably set it up this way.... So no one can do anything except stay lost. You are probably in cahoots with the devil himself she responds shaking her head and pointing her finger.

"Fuck you bitch", she replies as she walks away from her.

"Don't you turn your back on me... You slut", she says.

"FUCK YOU", she yells as she heads for her and puts her fingers around Missy's throat and starts squeezing.

"What.... It’s not bad enough you have doomed us to eternity in hell, now you want to kill me yourself?" Missy says as her head grows light.

Releasing her grip on her throat, she says, "I'm sorry... I don't know what came over me", as she starts to cry.

"That's all right... It's my fault. If I hadn't said what I did, we wouldn't be fighting like this. I'm sorry. It's just that we are both tired and hungry. Let's try to be a little more bearable... Okay?"

"Okay", she says in between sobs.

"Okay. Let's go get'em", Missy says as she starts to smile.

Getting over her crying jag, Tabrinia gets up and follows after her. Rounding a corner, they come face to face with four of the creatures. Seeing them, the things start roaring. Screaming as they turn and run, they run smack into Kensing and knock him over as they say, "Quick... Close the doorway", as a creature starts coming through the doorway.

Powering the system down, the creature roars in pain as half of its body is chopped off, as the doorway closes. Going over to Tabrinia, Terrin hugs her and they relate what happened as best they can. Opening the doorway back up, they toss the creature back through and power the system off.

"I thought for a minute there, we were going to be having company", Terrin says.

"We almost did", Tabrinia says as she smiles at Terrin.

Seeing the food, Tabrinia and Missy both start eating the food up. "Man am I hungry", Missy says as she digs in and starts stuffing her face full.

Talking and getting up to date on what has been happening, they all tell what happened with them in hell. Going back upstairs, Terrin locks the lab up as they all go into the house and go to bed. Sleeping soundly for the first few hours, everyone starts having dreams at the same time. Thing is, they are also having the same dream as each other. They also see everyone else there to.

Waking up the next morning, Tanya, Tabrinia and Missy start getting breakfast ready. Drinking a couple cups of coffee while making breakfast, they go and wake the guys up. "Hey... Babe... Time to get up. Breakfast is ready", Tabrinia says as she whispers and blows into his ear.

Waking up, he opens his eyes and smiles as he sees Tabrinia's beautiful face. "I'll be down in a couple of minutes", he yawns as he sits up in bed.

Trying to kiss him, he pulls away and says something about morning breath. Going back into the kitchen, Tabrinia makes sure everything is ready. Getting out of bed, Terrin puts some shorts on. Walking into the kitchen as he blinks the sleep out of his eyes, Terrin looks at the table and smiles. "Nice..... Very nice", he says as he smiles.

"Thanks", they all say together.

Walking in Kensing looks at everyone and says, "Mornin".

"Mornin' bud", Terrin replies.

"Good morning", Tabrinia and Missy say together.

"What's so good about it", Kensing replies sarcastically as Terrin and him start to laugh.

"Shut up and just sit down", Tabrinia replies in a playful manner.

Eating breakfast in relative silence with little or no talk going on, they finish and discuss what they are going to do today. "I figured we could help Kensing get a lab of his own set up in the basement. Maybe he can come up with some way to find an antidote for the drug he has made", Terrin says.

"Yeah.... Missy and me have been trying to. We had a discussion last night and talked about some issues that have been nagging at the both of us", Kensing says.

"Well... First thing is to clean the basement and see where he wants to put everything", Tabrinia says.

"Let's take a look", Kensing says as he gets up and leaves the table.

Following him, they all go downstairs. Except Tanya, who stays and starts cleaning up. Once downstairs, Kensing tells them where he wants everything. Nodding as he agrees, Terrin goes back upstairs and gets the cleaning things. Coming back down, Kensing follows him outside as the girls start cleaning the place up.

Going over to the truck Kensing and Missy drove up, they start unloading the contents. As the day wears on, they get the lab set up. Getting his computer online and working, Kensing starts running some data specs. Getting Missy to run some tests on their DNA, she makes up some special, liquid stuff for them. "Hey Terrin... Do you know where we can get a few animals for our experiments?" Kensing asks.

"No. I don't know where anything is at here. Tabrinia might know. Hang on let me ask her", Terrin replies.

Going upstairs he asks her if she knows where to find an animal store. Not knowing, she shrugs her shoulders. Going back downstairs he tells Kensing they don't know. Looking at his watch, Terrin sees it is 7:43 p.m. Heading back upstairs he grabs Tabrinia and leads her to the bedroom.

Making love to her for a few hours, they fall asleep afterward. Meanwhile, downstairs Tanya is in the basement with Kensing and Missy. Doing what they ask she fills up beakers and heats up other things they need. Finally, satisfied with the way the lab looks Kensing says, "Now this is what I call a lab", as he smiles at the girls.

Setting up his next set of tests, Tanya runs upstairs and uses the bathroom. Going to the computer Kensing runs a batch of numbers through it for confirmation. Waiting for the computer to finish, he takes some samples and starts running some other tests. Coming back downstairs Tanya goes back to what she was doing.

Waking up at 6:00 a.m., Terrin and Tabrinia head to the kitchen for coffee. Making a pot they hear a lot of noise coming from downstairs. Going to the door he opens it and they go down. Looking around as they get to the bottom of the stairs, they see an elaborate laboratory all set up and in operation.

"What the hell is all the noise down here?" Terrin asks still sleepy.

"We have been running some tests and getting things done I should have gotten done sooner", Kensing replies as he looks up and smiles.

"Damn... You make enough noise to wake up the dead", Terrin replies as he starts to smile.

"You are such an asshole", Kensing whispers to him.

"No more than you", Terrin replies.

Shaking his head he continues with what he was doing as Terrin and Tabrinia go back upstairs. Sitting down at the kitchen table, Terrin lets Tabrinia get his coffee for him. Thinking about what he needs to do so he can get his experiment up and running, he figures he will get his dishes up today.

As she sets his coffee down in front of him he looks up and smiles. "So... What are your plans for today babe?" she asks him.

"I was wanting to get my dishes installed. I want to check out the rest of the doorways potential. The other doorway we had before, has to be a lot better than the one we have been in", he says.

"Sounds like a winner to me", she says smiling

at him.

Drinking their coffee they finish off two cups each and then go outside to get started on the dishes. Getting everything out of the truck, Terrin starts hooking cables and other wires up to all the dishes. Getting them ready to be installed, he finishes with the last one and looks at his watch. Seeing it is 1:37 p.m., he asks Tabrinia if she can make something for lunch because he was starving.

Agreeing to it, she goes inside and starts making lunch for them. Walking around the house Terrin looks for the most promising location to install the dishes at. Finding a tree with the perfect place, he starts carrying the dishes over to the tree. Tying ropes around three of the dishes, he starts climbing with one of the dishes slung over his back.

Getting to the top of the tree, he starts cleaning branches out of the way. Getting the spot ready for the dishes, he starts mounting the first one to the tree. Setting it up and then checking the position it is pointing in, he gets it lined up with what he had before. Getting it just right, he starts pulling another dish up. Getting it in position, he wipes the sweat off his forehead.

Getting the next one up and ready and the last one done he climbs down and starts running cables to the lab. While running the cables, Tabrinia came out and told him lunch was ready. Going in to eat he talks with Tabrinia and they discuss what they have been doing on their experiment.

"So... We know it's a doorway. We know it

goes to hell… If we don't have the dishes hooked up to it properly. We just don't know where the original doorway took us. I mean the dog couldn't talk and always wanted to go back. Maybe it's a doorway to the future, or other planets we don't know about", he says as he sits back and drinks a cup of coffee.

"Maybe it was heaven?" Tabrinia suggests as she starts smiling and giggling.

"Yeah right. A doorway to GOD. That's good", he replies as he breaks out into laughter.

"Yeah... And we could be the best ever preachers in the world… Cause we have a doorway to GOD", she says as she breaks out into laughter with him.

Coming up the stairs Kensing, Tanya and Missy come into the kitchen looking tired. As they come in, they all look at Terrin and Tabrinia and ask, "What's so damn funny?"

"Nothing", Tabrinia replies as her and Terrin start laughing more.

"Come on... What gives? Don't keep us in the dark anymore... Please", Kensing says as they burst out laughing.

"Okay... We were talking about the doorway… And where it went originally", Terrin tells them.

"Okay... I myself think it was hell", Kensing says.

"We already agreed on that one... We were talking about when we first had it going in Colorado. The dog we put through it always wanted to go back. So we started coming up with where it could lead. She", as he nods towards Tabrinia, "thought it went to heaven...

No wait... That's GOD. Then she said we could be the best preachers in the world, cause we had a doorway to GOD", he says as they start breaking out in laughter.

"That has got to be the best one I ever heard of", Kensing says as he laughs some more.

"Oh shut up and go to bed", Tabrinia says as she turns around.

CHAPTER 10

Going to their rooms Kensing, Tanya and Missy crash for awhile. When they are gone Tabrinia says, "Did you have to tell them that it was my idea?" as she playfully punches him in the arm.

"I'm sorry", as he gives her his special puppy-dog eyes. Then they both burst out into laughter.

"C'mon", as he gets up and heads out the door.

Following Terrin outside he tells her he needs to get the rest of the cables run so he can get the doorway operational again. Helping him get the cables run, they finally get them run into the lab. Hooking them up where they go, Terrin soon has his doorway working like before, but a little different. Shaking his head as he sees the readings he is getting as he takes a sheet of paper and compares them with what is coming up on the computer.

"What's wrong?" Tabrinia asks him.

"Something's wrong with the figures from Colorado to here", as he tries to explain.

"Maybe it's the location. It could have a different effect because we are at a different place, therefore, at a different magnetic pull", she offers.

Shaking his head up and down he says, "Yeah. That could be the ticket", as he starts up the stairs and heads out of the lab.

"What?" she asks as she follows him.

"Hang on", as he goes into the house and goes downstairs.

Rummaging around he can't seem to find what he is looking for. "Hey Tab. Have you seen a brown crate with the letters KNIGHTWARP on it?"

"Yeah... When we were cleaning the place up, I took it up to the attic. Why?" she asks curiously.

Running up the stairs he heads for the attic. Pulling the stairs down he climbs up and finds the case. Grabbing it he takes it down and puts the stairs back up. Hauling it to the lab Tabrinia follows him. Getting down to the lab he puts it on a table and opens it. Pulling out a micro-magnetic stabilizer field generator, he turns it on and adjusts it for the difference in magnetic pull.

Going over to the control panel he opens the doorway again. Hearing a slightly different pitch in the electrical current, he goes over to the computer and looks at the figures and compares them with the other figures. Nodding his head a little bit, he goes back and readjusts the field generator. Going back to the computer he nods his head and smiles. "YES".

"I take it you've got it?" she asks querulously.

"Yes. We did it. The same readings as in

Colorado", he replies as he goes over and hugs her.

Hugging him back she smiles and says, "It's about time something made you happy".

Pulling away from her he asks, "What are you talking about? You make me happy".

"Yeah... But not like this... This", as she waves at the machines and computers, "stuff can".

"That's bull and you know it", he says. "You make me damn happy. I love you more than you'll ever know", as a tear come to his eye.

"Well... You never show it anymore. You're always down here taking care of your 'doorway' as you call it", she explains. "It's like… I can't please you the way this stuff does".

"Babe. That's not true. You always please me with everything you do. What will it take to make you believe me?" he asks.

"Show me that you love me… Like you say you do and give up your stuff for awhile. Is that too much to ask?"

"No it's not. How about tomorrow you and me? We'll take a ride out and see if we can find a swimming hole and have a picnic?" he suggests.

Looking at him and smiling she says, "Okay.... I like that idea", as she kisses him.

Breaking apart he continues with his experiment, while Tabrinia goes upstairs and gets things ready for tomorrow. Getting all the settings just right, Terrin starts thinking about some kind of device so he would be able to see the doorway from the other side. Trying to come up with something viable, his mind is a blank.

Closing the doorway he goes to the computer and poses the question to the computer. "I'm sorry. But the question you asked is not in my data banks", the computer says in a very masculine voice.

"What the hell was that", Terrin asks to himself as there is no one else down there with him.

Putting his hand on the mouse, he looks through various files and finds what he is looking for. Opening the program up was looking for, he starts it. "Good evening Terrin", a rather exciting feminine voice says. "Feeling horny tonight?' it asks.

"Always..... Jennifer", he replies as he starts laughing.

"Good. Now... What can I do for you?"

Asking her the question he had asked a few minutes ago, she says it will take a little time. But that she should have an answer by 9:47 p.m. tonight. Shaking his head up and down he starts trying to do some rough calculations of his own. Using another projection form of his field, he has an idea that may just work. Getting together some of the things he has been using as stand-by equipment, he starts integrating some of his particular micro-magnetic engineering electronics into a hand held remote control.

Taking the remote apart, he sees what has to be done until he gets his answer. Modifying the remote control he starts putting things in and taking certain other things out. Just then, Tabrinia comes down and says, "Terrin babe.... It's time for dinner".

"Bring it down here. I am in the middle of

getting something great done. I need some time, plus the computer is doing some calculations for me. If that is all right?" as he looks at her in a meek way.

Smiling she says, "Okay... I will let it slide… This time", as she runs up the stairs and goes back into the house.

Going back to the remote, he finishes up what he was doing when she comes down and brings him his dinner. "Here you are babe. London broil... Rare.... But not too rare... Baked potato and corn. And, if you use your imagination you can almost guess what is for dessert", as she smiles at him sexily.

"All right. That sounds great," as he takes the proffered plate.

Sitting down in front of the computer, they both watch as the computer finishes its computations. Seeing the results, Terrin smiles as he says, "My thinking exactly".

Looking at him strangely she asks, "What?"

"I figured basically the same thing. The only thing I didn't figure on, was the figure here. I couldn't get it to come out right", he explains.

"Oh, I see", she replies.

Going back to the remote he was working on, he puts the rest of the modifications into it. Using a special tool, he starts readjusting the bandwidth.

When Terrin and Tabrinia went in and were looking for his crate, they woke Kensing up. Getting out of bed he goes into the bathroom and brushes his teeth after using the facilities.

Coming out of the bathroom, he walks into the kitchen and makes a cup of coffee. Walking to the door downstairs, he goes down and closes the door behind him.

Once he can open his eyes and concentrate on what he is doing, he starts running some tests that no one else will know about. Getting some samples from himself, he is trying to find a drug that is dedicated to the DNA host. In other words, it won't work for anyone else except the person it was designed for.

Getting results that are fascinating and exciting, he gets to a point where he can stop and pick up the next night. Putting everything away he shuts everything off and goes back to his room. Getting into bed he falls asleep within minutes.

Once he had the bandwidth where he wanted it, he went over and sat down next to Tabrinia and finished eating. Looking over at Tabrinia, he sees her smiling at him. Smiling back she takes his hand and leads him over to a table. Putting the remote down as she takes his hand, he lets her lead him over to the table.

Sitting on the top, she takes her top off and underneath she is wearing a sexy, red teddy. Smiling as he sees what she has in mind, he starts taking his shirt off. Getting his shirt off he starts kissing her. Kissing him back she wraps her arms around his body. Massaging her breasts as he kisses her, she starts unzipping his pants. Moving his hand down he starts taking her shorts down.

Putting her hand into his underwear as his pants fall down around his ankles, she smiles and starts rubbing on his crotch. Getting her shorts off, he puts his hand in her crotch. Putting his fingers up and into her, they make love on top of the table. When they finish, they turn everything off and go upstairs to the house and then to bed. Falling asleep as their heads hit the pillows, they sleep until the next morning.

CHAPTER 11

When Terrin and Tabrinia woke up they went into the other rooms wake the others up. When they all see what time it is, they got out of bed and went downstairs to the kitchen for their coffee. Getting things ready in the kitchen Kensing goes downstairs and starts getting everything ready for the day ahead. When the girls finally come down, he is running some tests and has the results that were printed out while they slept.

Handing them to Missy he says, "I don't like the results. We can come up with a lot better results than that", with a disgusted sound to his voice.

"I'm trying everything I can.... It just takes a little time and some trial and error", she says trying to calm him down.

"I know... It's just that we need to get the better results as soon as possible. If we can get some satisfactory results.... I may be able to come up with an antidote to the patches", Kensing says trying to explain why he needed it so bad.

"I'll do what I can. I can't promise miracles, but I can sure as hell try my best", as she smiles at him.

Smiling back at her, they all go back to running tests and getting the wrong results. Getting closer as the night wears on, they finally come up with some very promising results. Smiling as they all agree that they are closer than they've ever been, they all take a break. Going upstairs Missy and Tanya get some champagne and glasses. Going back downstairs they show Kensing what they got and he nods his head and smiles.

Popping the cork on one of the bottles, Missy pours some in each glass. Raising his glass in a toast, Kensing says, "To the success that we will encounter sooner. Thanks to Tanya and Missy.... To two people who made it possible, to get as far as we have. May all your results produce the same satisfactory results we have been seeing here tonight. Thanks you two", as he clinks his glass with theirs.

As they all drink up and finish off the bottle, they go back to running some more advanced tests. Getting some better results, Missy goes over and alters a few miniscule items that she neglected to take into consideration. Running the tests again, she comes up with even better results than Kensing ever thought possible. Taking the data sheet over to him, he screams out in triumph, "YES".

"What?" Tanya asks.

"The results are better than I ever hoped for.

This is a major break-through... Do you realize what this means?" he asks incredulously.

"It means we can finally break this habit, without upsetting the changes we have already undergone?" Missy asks.

"Yes... But how did you know?" Kensing asks.

"When I was running the tests, I got to thinking, what would happen if I started doing different modifications and what the consequences would be. Well.... It hit me as soon as the results came back. I couldn't believe it was possible either", she says as she grins the biggest grin she has ever had.

Patting her on the back he says, "We have made some vast improvements tonight. I say, lets all go to bed and get plenty of rest so we can finish this part of the experiment. We deserve it. Let's go", as they turn the lights out and go upstairs to bed.

Looking at his watch, Kensing sees it is six a.m. Yawning as he goes into his bedroom, he closes the door and lies down on the bed. Getting back up a few minutes later, he sets his alarm clock for three in the afternoon. Lying back down on the bed, he falls asleep and has some rather bizarre dreams.

Waking up, around six-thirty, Terrin and Tabrinia go in and take a shower together. Getting out of the shower and drying each other off, they get dressed and ready for the day ahead. After getting dressed, Tabrinia goes downstairs and makes some coffee and breakfast. When Terrin comes down, she has breakfast and coffee ready for him and on the table.

Smiling as he enters the kitchen he says, "Now this is the way to wake up", as he sits down and takes a drink of his coffee.

"Good morning babe", as she smiles at him sexily.

"Good morning to you, too, sexy", he smiles back at her.

Sitting down next to him, they eat breakfast and talk about the day ahead. Laughing and having a great time as they relive some old times they both remember, she punches him every now and then in the shoulder. Not too hard though. Finishing breakfast, they clean up the dishes and wash them. Getting the place the way it was when they came in, they get their things together and head out to his truck. Putting the stuff in, they jump in and he starts it up.

Letting it idle for about five minutes, he turns the radio on and listens to some light rock. Putting the truck in drive, he gives it some gas and they are on their way. Driving out into the pasture they own, they follow a track that looks like it used to be well traveled. Driving for a couple of hours, they finally get to the end of the tracks.

It is the most beautiful sight. A nice little romantic waterfall, that falls about twenty feet. A little pond at the base that is about seventy-five feet across. Pointing at a spot that looks just right, they go over and set up their picnic. Sitting down next to Tabrinia, Terrin starts taking her clothes off. "Hey... What the hell are you doing?"

she asks in a playful voice.

"I'm getting you ready to go swimming", he replies as he continues taking her clothes off.

"Really. Then I guess I will have to get you ready", as she starts taking his clothes off.

Stripping each other down, Terrin picks Tabrinia up and throws her into the pond. Grabbing around his neck as he does, she pulls him in too. Laughing as they come up for air, Terrin says, "This brings back some memories".

"Yeah, it does", she says, swimming over to him.

Taking her in his arms, he starts kissing her. Kissing him back, she pulls away and says, "Let's go over their", as she points across the water.

Nodding his head "Okay... Last one over is a rotten egg", as he swims away.

Swimming after him, she catches up and then passes him. Getting there first she smiles and says, "I guess you are the rotten egg".

"I guess so", as they burst out laughing.

Standing on the bottom, he picks her up and kisses her. Kissing him back, she starts doing things to him that only she is allowed to do. Making love in the water, they finish and just swim around and talk about where they want to be this time next year. As the day wears on, they swim back over to their blanket and sit down.

Getting the food out and ready to eat, he makes sandwiches. Dishing stuff out as he gets the sandwiches ready, she puts his plate down in front of him. Getting her sandwich finished, he puts it on her plate. Making one for him, he finishes and picks up his plate. Talking in between bites, they finish the conversation she started on the other side.

Getting finished, they lay back and close their eyes. Lying there in the nude, they fall asleep and have rather pleasant dreams about their lives. Sleeping soundly for what seems hours but is only an hour, Terrin wakes up and as he rolls over he falls into the water. Shaking his head, he starts laughing and pulls Tabrinia in with him. Waking up rather rudely, she comes up for air and can't help but smile, as she looks at Terrin.

Smiling back he says, "That was a hell of a way to wake up", as he explains to her what happened to him.

Laughing as he finishes, she can't help herself. Swimming backwards, away from him, she makes it to the other side before he can catch her. Walking under the waterfall, she waits to see if he will come up here. Turning around, he is standing behind her, startling her. Punching him playfully, she says, "Don't ever sneak up on me, like that again".

"Taking her in his arms, he says, "Okay my darling", as he plants a kiss on her lips before she can say anymore.

Kissing him back they proceed to make love, right there, under the waterfall. You couldn't ask for a more romantic night, than the night they were having.

Waking up at noon, Kensing walks downstairs and gets some coffee. Making his coffee, he goes down to the basement and starts on his secret project. As he gets all his stuff together, he finishes his tests that he was in the middle of the last time. Nodding his head, he starts making some of the formula that the computer had come up with.

He makes the mix and then starts thinning out the liquid, but making it stronger than usual. Getting the right consistency, he shakes his head up and down in approval. Hearing a noise upstairs, he puts everything away, as fast as possible. Getting the last sample in the cabinet and just moving away from it, Tanya comes down and asks, "What's going on?"

"Nothing. I couldn't sleep and decided to come down and check everything out", Kensing replies.

"Oh... I thought maybe there were burglars down here", as she yawns. "But seeing as how I am awake, I might as well get to work", she adds as she goes upstairs and gets some coffee.

While the coffee brews, Tanya wakes Missy up and then goes into the bathroom for a shower. Turning the water on, she starts opening her eyes, a little at a time. Washing her body she reflects on all that has happened since she came here.

As she rinses her hair, she turns the water off and gets out. Drying her body off, she wraps the towel around her and goes to her room. Getting dressed, she comes out and hears Missy in the shower. Smiling to herself, she goes into the kitchen and gets something for breakfast.

By the time Missy is out of the shower, Tanya has breakfast ready and waiting. Smiling, as she comes in and smells the food, she says, "Smells wonderful", as she sniffs again.

Going to the door to the basement, Tanya yells out, "Kensing... Time to eat".

Turning around, she hears him saying, okay. Going to the table, she sits down and starts dishing food onto her plate. Coming up the stairs, Kensing comes over and sits down next to Missy. Dishing his plate up, he starts eating. Making small talk and trying to get everyone in the mood for work, he talks about what they need to do, now that they have the figures and data on the antidote.

Agreeing with him, they all nod in unison. They eat in relative silence, except when someone needs something. Finishing the breakfast, they all thank Tanya and go downstairs. Cleaning the dishes up, she goes into the kitchen and washes them as well. Getting done cleaning up she makes the place look like it did before breakfast, she finishes and goes downstairs.

Continuing with her part of the experiment, she finds some amazing results of her own. Taking them over to Kensing, he tells her what a great job she has done and to keep up the excellent work. Nodding her head and going back, she is happy to be praised for what she did. She was actually blushing, as she thought about it.

CHAPTER 12

Starting on some more tests, she starts changing things, to see what the effects are. Writing down all the effects, as she gets the results, she notices one set, had a very familiar order to them. Taking them over to Kensing, she hands him the pages and explains what she thinks it is. Nodding his head in agreement, he takes the results over and asks Missy what she thinks.

Agreeing with them, Tanya goes ahead and takes the one set and makes a sample drug. Integrating it into the other drug and seeing what it does, she notices something odd. Shaking her head as she realizes what it is, she continues with what she was doing. Mixing the two together and running the results in the computer, it tells her, it will take a little bit. Please be patient.

Nodding her head, she goes over and starts even more tests. Changing first one thing, then another, she gets the results she is hoping for. Going back to the computer, she sees it is still working on the problem. Running upstairs, she uses the bathroom. Doing her business, she goes back out and gets another cup of coffee.

As she heads back downstairs after getting her coffee, she sees the computer is done. Checking the results, she sees exactly what she was hoping to find. Taking the paper over to Kensing, he gives her a big hug and tells her to take the rest of the day off. Thanking him, she goes upstairs and goes into her room.

Falling across her bed, she decides to get up and go for a walk. Feeling like a rotten daughter, cause she has been spending all her time with Kensing, instead of her Dad, she starts crying, hoping he won't hate her. Kicking herself in the butt, she reprimands herself and decides, from now on, she is going to spend more time with him. As she walks around, she glances at her watch and sees it is 5:00 a.m.

Just about time to go to bed. Maybe she could take a nap and try to wake up, for when her Dad and Tabrinia started work. Maybe she could help them, in some way. Repay them, for everything they have done. Walking back into the house, she goes into her room and lies down after setting her clock for 9:00 a.m.

After they made love under the waterfall, they swam back to the other side and lay down. Cuddling in each other's arms, they fall asleep. Sleeping soundly through the night, they wake up at about 6:00 a.m., as she shivers, from not having any clothes on. As Terrin gets a fire going they warm up, as the water for coffee warms up.

Jumping into the water, Terrin splashes around and says, "C'mon in... The waters nice and warm, compared to the air".

Testing the water with her foot, she feels it is nice. Jumping in, she shivers and says, "You asshole... It's freezing", as she shivers.

Going over to her, he is laughing as he gets near. Cuddling with her and trying to get her warmed up, he says, "You have to move to keep warm".

"Okay... We'll see", as she splashes him with water.

Going under, he comes up under her and pulls her legs down. Screaming as she is pulled down, she swims away. Going after her, after coming up for air, he finally catches her and grabs her and takes her in his arms. Kissing her deeply, as they hold each other, they swim towards shore.

Once they get to where Terrin can stand up, he does and holds her up too. Reaching down, he... You know what he did... And then afterwards, they swam back to the blanket and got dried off and dressed. Getting some coffee for them, Tabrinia takes a cup over to Terrin. As she hands it to him, "Here you go babe", as she smiles.

"Thanks darling", he replies as he smiles at her.

Taking a sip, he says, "Hey... This is great... What kind is it?"

"Same thing we have been drinking... Except that the water is different", she explains.

"Tastes great. I don't care if it is the water", he

replies as he sits down.

Sitting down next to him, they look out over the pond and think. "You know.... This would be the perfect spot for a nice little house", he says in a romantic sort of voice.

"Yeah", she replies in a dreamy voice of her own.

Cuddling up with him after setting her coffee down, she wraps her arms around his arms and just snuggles with him.

As Kensing and Missy run the new figures that Tanya came up with, they find some very astonishing discoveries. "Kensing... This is what you have been looking for", Missy says.

"What 'we', have been looking for", he replies.

"Okay... We... Will it work, like you thought it would?" she asks.

"I believe it should. If the calculations are right, it should do what we wanted from it".

"I can't believe we have done what we have done, in so short a time. I always thought the scientists and doctors were always lying to us, about it taking so long to do something".

"Like I have always told you.... They are not in it for the science, but the money", he replies to her, as he goes over and turns her around to face him. "Missy... I.... I'm not sure what to say... Except that maybe, I am very sorry for what I did to you.... It's just that... Well..... I love you, and want to spend all my life with you... I did it, because I love you", as tears come to his eyes. "Can you ever forgive me?"

As tears form in the corner of her eyes, "Yes...

I can forgive you... I never knew you cared about me so much", she replies in an awestruck voice.

"I have always loved you. It's just that, I didn't know it, until we started hanging out together".

"And I was falling for you, the more time I spent around you. I guess if I would have stayed, I would be miserable right now. So yes, I do forgive you", she says as she hugs him.

Hugging her back, he wipes the tears away, as best he can. Pulling slightly away from her, he looks into her eyes and can see the love and adoration deep down. Smiling, he brings his face closer to hers and kisses her gently and tenderly. Kissing him back, they stay lip-locked for about five minutes.

Breaking away, they continue with their research. "Missy... Run me that emotion stabilizer test, on the newest formula and see what it says. If it's right, we should have the results that I have been telling you about", Kensing says in his usual, business manner.

"Okay... I'm on it", she replies as she gets busy.

Going back to his own tests, he finds a few new things he hadn't seen before. Noticing that it will also have a positive effect, with his newest and yet untold formula. Sneaking a little bit of it away, he goes to where he keeps his secret project going. Pouring it into the mixture he has already placed inside, he stirs it up and then closes the cabinet.

Going back to the project at hand, he makes small talk with Missy. Looking at his watch, he sees it is 8:30 a.m., and time to go to bed. Going over to Missy he says, "Time to hit the sack. Ready?"

"Yeah... Let me finish this real quick", as she puts the last of her figures into the computer and gets it working.

Letting him lead her upstairs, he takes her into his room. Kissing her neck and starting to take her shirt off, she turns around and starts undressing him.

After having two cups of coffee each and another dip Terrin and Tabrinia head back to the house. Looking back, she has a sad face, as the pond dwindles away. Looking over at her and seeing her long face, he says, "Don't worry... We'll be back", as he squeezes her leg.

"I know", she says as she starts smiling again.

Driving back and remembering the great time they had, Terrin says they will come back this weekend and bring Tanya with them. Agreeing with him, she smiles and hugs him. Pulling into the yard at 8:57 a.m., they drive up and stop the truck. Getting out and helping Tabrinia out, they go into the house.

Going over to the basement door, Terrin looks down and doesn't see any lights on. Closing the door, he says, "They must all be sleeping again. I can't believe they stay up and work all night and sleep all day. But then again... That is the way Kensing always was, when I knew him", he laughs, as he smiles, remembering the times they used to have.

"How about if I make some breakfast?" she asks.

"That would be great", as he smiles. "I am going to take a shower while you do", as he kisses her on his way out of the kitchen.

Kissing him back, he runs into Tanya on the way. "Mornin' sleepy head", he says to her, as he smiles.

"Mornin' Dad", she says, as she hugs him. "I'm sorry I haven't been spending any time with you. Can you ever forgive me?" as she starts crying.

"Hey babe... You don't have anything to be sorry for. No matter what you do or what you say... I will always love you and care about you. So yes, I will always forgive you", he replies, as he hugs her real tight.

"Oh Dad... Thanks", she says as she bursts out into tears.

Leading her into the bathroom, he sits down on the toilet and sets her on his lap. "You are my baby. You mean a lot more to me than words or actions", he tells her as he cries with her.

Sniffling, as they try to hold back the rest of the tears, she asks, "Can I come down and help you out?"

"Anytime you want to. I would love it", he says. "Oh...... By the way... Tabrinia and I went and found a killer pond, with a waterfall. We were thinking about spending next weekend down there and camp. You game?" he asks.

"I would love it", she says, as she hugs him and then gets up. "I am going to make you a breakfast you will never forget", as she smiles and starts to leave.

"You will have to beat Tabrinia to it then", he

laughs as he smiles back at her.

"Damn", stomping her foot as she heads to the kitchen.

CHAPTER 13

Getting into the kitchen, she sees Tabrinia just starting breakfast. "Mornin' ", Tanya says, all smiles.

"Good morning", Tabrinia replies.

"Can I help?" Tanya asks.

"Yeah... Come on... Jump in... That would be great", Tabrinia says as she starts getting some eggs scrambled.

Helping her out, she gets the bacon and sausage ready and the toast done, as Tabrinia gets the eggs and pancakes done. Getting everything done and ready, they take it out to the dining room and set it up. As they get done setting the last thing down, Terrin walks in and smiles and says, "So... How are the two most beautiful women in the world today?" as he sits down between Tanya and Tabrinia.

"Fine", Tanya says.

"Just great", Tabrinia replies as she smiles at him.

"I'm wonderful... Today, I have turned another page in my life", as he smiles at Tanya.

Smiling back at him Tanya says, "Dad".

"What", as he raises his eyebrows.

"Oh nothing", as she blushes.

Tabrinia looks at them, and gives him a puzzled look. "I'm lost", she says.

"My daughter has come back to me, for good", Terrin says, smiling like the proud father he is.

"Oh", Tabrinia says as she continues eating.

Once they have breakfast done, Terrin kisses both of them and heads to the lab. Getting the kitchen and dining room cleaned, Tanya and Tabrinia wash everything and clean up their mess. When they get done, they go down and join Terrin in the lab.

Once down in the lab, Terrin turns his equipment on and checks for any leaks or electrical problems. Turning the computer on, he waits for it to warm up. As it comes on and the programs start running, it says, "Good morning Terrin. So, how was your sex last night?" in a feminine voice.

Blushing to himself, he says, "None of your damn business Jennifer", as he starts laughing. "I can't believe this. A computer that asks about your sex life. What a world we live in", mumbling, as he continues laughing. "Jennifer... I need you to run the computations we ran the last time, but reduce the tri-x factor and increase the electrical through-put, in box 211-A.I need the results, as fast as you can. I have a very good feeling about this", as he gets his remote and starts modifying it again.

"The answer will be ready in one hour, forty eight minutes and thirteen seconds", the computer replies as it begins working on the latest data.

Adjusting the tri-temporal stimulator, Terrin checks the results and likes what he sees. Using a gas stabilizer limitation armature, he hooks it up into his remote and checks to see if it works. Working like it was designed to, he smiles and continues making adjustments with his new information.

Getting done with the remote for now, he puts it down and looks up to see the girls coming down the stairs. Smiling, he says, "Ready for some real work?"

"Ready and waiting", they both say in unison, as they start laughing, (must be a girl thing), Terrin thinks.

Getting them started on some other things he needs done, he starts the system up. Looking at the gauges that are arranged around the control panel, he sees one he doesn't like. Tapping the glass front, it stays in the same place. Shutting the system down, he says, "Tabrinia... Give me a hand for a minute... Will you?"

"Be right there", she says as she puts her pad down and goes over to him.

Lifting doorway hatch "B" up, he tells her what she needs to do. Feeling around in there, she feels what he described and tugs on it. Not budging it, she says, "I can't seem to get it to move".

"Oh... To the right of it, is a release button. You have five seconds to remove the capacitance resistor module, before the locks reactivate", he tells her.

Feeling to the right of it, she feels something that doesn't seem right. Feeling, just to be sure, she says, "I think your system got fried. It feels like a bunch of wires all burned together".

"Damn... I was afraid of that", he says. "That's all right. Go back to what you were doing. I need to take the whole thing apart to fix the damn thing... Shit", he says as he stands up and playfully kicks it.

Going over to the tool cabinet, he gets what he needs and start dismantling the doorway. Looking at his watch, he sees it is already 11:30 a.m. Shaking his head, he mumbles to himself, 'There's never enough time for anything'.

"Did you say something?" Tabrinia asks.

"Just talking to myself", he replies as he looks around at her and smiles.

Smiling back as she sees him peek around the corner, she turns around and starts on some new tests. Getting the panel off, he looks inside the machine and says, "Son of a bitch... What the hell got in here and tore the shit up?" to no one in particular.

Coming over to him, Tanya and Tabrinia ask, "What", as they look inside and see the mess.

"Someone, or something, has gotten in here and sabotaged my experiment", he says sounding a little baffled.

"Are you sure it couldn't have been because of the electrical storm we had, the night the power went out and we all got stuck?" Tabrinia asks.

"I don't think so. This looks like something someone has done. But who?" he asks.

"No one I know", Tabrinia shrugs.

"Don't look at me", Tanya replies as she puts her hands up, in a defensive posture.

Shaking his head, he tells them they can go back with what they were doing. Getting some more tools, he goes over and starts replacing the burnt wiring. Checking all the modules and terminators, he finds two bad ones and replaces them, with higher input voltage frequencies. Getting the doorway back together, he starts the system again. Looking at the dials and gauges, he sees all the readings within tolerable conditions, (by his standards).

Opening the doorway, he jumps through and looks around. Liking what he sees, he jumps back into the lab. "That is so cool", he exclaims, as he comes back through.

"What is?" Tabrinia asks, as she looks up at him.

Pointing at the doorway, he says, "What's through the doorway... It's like clouds... But not like them... It's nice and comfortable... But not too comfortable... It's different", he explains. "Here... See for yourself".

Jumping into the doorway, she looks around and sees what he saw. Gaping in awe as she sees what he was talking about, Tanya bumps into her, as she comes through. "Wow", she says.

"This is definitely cool as hell", Tabrinia says.

"I'm tellin' ya", Tanya replies, as she agrees with her.

Going back into the lab, they both agree with Terrin and what he said. "I told you. Isn't it beautiful", he asks?

"Definitely gorgeous", they both say in unison as they burst out laughing.

"Okay... Let's get busy, so we can go and explore this new place".

Grabbing his remote, he starts tinkering with the switches and dials he has added. Checking the bandwidth frequency, he changes it just slightly. Nodding his head, he goes over and talks to the computer. "Jennifer... Where are my results?" he asks.

"They have been done for one hour and twenty-five minutes and", the computer starts saying.

"Jennifer... Jennifer.... I just want the results and nothing else. Okay?'

"They are ready", she says as if she had feelings and they were hurt.

"Jennifer... I'm sorry... I didn't mean to say it like that", he tries to explain.

"That's all right", the computer says in a snide tone as he thinks he almost hears a sob.

Grabbing the data sheets off the printer, he shakes his head and goes over to his workbench. Looking at the remote, he starts making the other adjustments the computer came up with. After making the necessary adjustments, he jumps through the doorway. As he jumps through, six of the components in the system malfunction. When the components burned out, they caused a small rift in the doorway.

Looking up as they are plunged into total darkness, Tabrinia finds the generator back up and gets it going. As the lights return to normal, Tabrinia asks the million-dollar question, "Where's Terrin?"

Looking around and not finding him, Tabrinia says, "You don't think", as she looks at the doorway.

"No way", Tanya says, as she looks at the doorway as well.

"There's only one way to find out", Tabrinia says as she goes over and turns the system on.

Looking at the gauges and dials, she sees three of them jumping erratically. And there are four lights, blinking on the control panel, also. "Oh shit", Tabrinia says.

"What?" Tanya asks.

"Something's wrong with the system. There's dials and gauges going crazy over here", she replies as she backs away from the console.

"Let me see", Tanya says as she comes over and looks at it.

"How much do you know about this?", Tabrinia asks her.

"Well... Let's just say I probably know more than my Dad", as she looks at her in her eye.

"Wow", Tabrinia replies as she shakes her head in approval.

Looking at the gauges, she starts saying, "We need to change four, triple-relay by-pass systems. 6 jumper capacitors and contactors... And for dessert, three tri-manifold relay adapters, with special spatial links systems onboard", as Tabrinia shakes her head.

"Whatever you said... I haven't got the slightest clue", she replies. "Just tell me what to do and I will do whatever I can to help".

"Okay... C'mon", as she leads her over to the doorway.

Taking things out and replacing them, she soon has the hardest components installed. Looking at her watch, she sees it is 6:00 p.m. "I'm hungry. How's about you going and getting something to eat and I will continue changing the parts out. Okay?" Tanya asks Tabrinia as she raises her eyebrow, just like her father.

Smiling, she says, "Yeah... Sure", as she runs up the stairs and heads to the kitchen.

Getting the next parts out and replaced she still has hours of work, before she is finished. Working as fast and efficiently as she can, she has two of the gyro-stabilized micro-magnetic relays changed by the time Tabrinia comes down with the food and drinks. Smiling as she comes down, Tanya goes over and starts eating and getting her fill.

"These are great", Tanya says as she takes a bite of the first sandwich.

"Thanks", Tabrinia replies as she starts eating too.

While they eat, they ponder over what really happened. Tanya tells her that the wiring was defective and that she had to change most of it out and upgrade the final strings of wire. Shaking her head, like she understands what Tanya is talking about, she continues eating.

CHAPTER 14

Jumping through the doorway, Terrin finds himself somewhere, besides where he was, a little bit ago. Going back the way he came from, he stays in the place he is at. Trying his remote, he starts to see a sort of glimmer, but he isn't sure if it's the remote, or his eyes. Shaking his head, trying to clear his vision, he activates it again and sees the same shimmering effect, as before.

Adjusting some of the bands, he tries it again. Not seeing anything, he turns the settings the opposite way. Trying it again, he sees the shimmering. Nodding his head, he adjusts two more of the dials and tries it again. Seeing the doorway as a red, shimmering, he says to himself, "YES".

Jumping up and down, he tries to activate the doorway. Nothing happens. Trying to adjust the remote to activate the doorway, he has no such luck. Walking around, he notices little green bugs that seem to be flying in clusters. Getting nearer to a cluster, he sees they are about six feet in height. Turning around, he hopes they don't see him and chase him. Walking away as he looks over his shoulder, he sees some of them coming.

Running away from them, they continue after him. Running like there is no tomorrow, he runs as fast as his long lanky legs will take him. Looking back over his shoulder, he sees them getting farther away. Stopping for a minute, he pants hard and tries to catch his breath. Watching the things they continue after him so he starts running again.

Remembering that he has the remote, he activates it and sees if there are any doorways around. Not seeing anything, he keeps running. Trying to run in a circle, he is soon so pooped, he has to stop and rest. As he stops, his stomach muscles clench together, from not eating and running so long.

Grabbing his stomach, he falls to the ground and lies there, trying to relax until his stomach will stop hurting. Finally, the pain subsides and he can move again. Looking at where the creatures were, he can't see them anymore. Trying the remote, he sees a red doorway, just up ahead, about two hundred feet away.

Walking toward it, he sees a group of the creatures coming, from a different direction. They are heading for the red doorway. Getting to the doorway, they look at it and try to go through it. Alas, they have no luck going through the doorway. Staying far enough away that they won't notice him, he waits to see if they leave.

All of a sudden, the doorway disappears and

the creatures are hitting each other and cussing, as they look for the doorway. Moving off, as a cloud of gnats would do, he waits a safe time, before getting up and heading for the doorway. Looking all around, he doesn't see any of those creatures around.

Activating the doorway, he is standing, not more than five feet from it. Trying to open the doorway, he steps through, hoping. As he steps through, he feels a different sensation, than when he first went through the doorway. Shivering as he looks around, he sees it looks like his lab. But it's all dirty and not in use. There are cobwebs, all over the place.

Knocking some of the cobwebs down, he looks at the machines and sees if there are any indications as to the last time it was fired up. Making his way over to the control panel, he looks down and sees the same basic design. Except for a few things he never had on his. Hitting the main switch, nothing happens.

Going to a door, he opens it up and looks at the gas gauge on the generator. Shaking his head, he tries to start the generator. It grinds slowly at first, then it starts to pick up some speed. Going back to the control panel, he hits the main switch again. As all the lights in the room come on, he is blinded momentarily, as his eyes adjust to the brightness.

Opening his eyes, he looks around and sees almost the same exact setup, as he had. Besides a few minor improvements he never got a chance to make. Checking the gauges and dials, they stay in the proper position. Shaking his head with approval, he opens the doorway. As it opens fully, all the sides roll down smoothly, as if they were new.

Once they are fully down and in position, he goes over and sticks his hand through the doorway, but it stays in the room. Going back to the control panel, he looks down at it. Shaking his head as if he is puzzled, he can't seem to fathom why the doorway won't open. Seeing a switch with no name, he presses it. As he presses the button, the doorway starts up and is fully functional.

"I never would have thought of a safeguard on the doorway", he says out loud.

Just then, one of the creatures comes through and spots Terrin. Looking around for anything to use as a weapon, he finds a lead pipe. Picking it up, he swings at the creature and knocks it back through the doorway. Going over to the control panel, he closes the doorway as another of the creature's starts to come through. When the doorway closed, it chopped whatever part of the creature was in the room off and the other part got left behind, in the other place.

Going over to the creature, Terrin raises the pipe, as the thing tries to grab for him. Smashing the creature's head in, it finally stops moving. Looking up, Terrin sees the good old computer sitting there, covered with dust. I thought it was gone, he thinks to himself. Going over to it, he finds a rag and starts dusting it off.

After getting all the dust off it, he turns it on and hopes it still works. Hearing the hard drive start up, he sees the monitor light up. "All right", he says to himself. Waiting for the system to boot up, he walks over to the control panel and turns some other systems off. Looking at the monitor, he sees half the programs are either damaged, or are not running.

Walking over to the computer, he clicks on the 'Jennifer' icon. Waiting, a message appears; Module 325 in section F11087 has been damaged and the program can't be run. Clicking on the OK button, the program finishes loading and a feminine voice says, "Have you had your snake today?" as it starts laughing.

"Jennifer.... Is that really you?" Terrin asks.

"Yes Terrin. It's the same old me, that you have been using for years now", the computer replies.

"Jennifer... I have a problem..... What is today's date?" Terrin asks.

"Today is Friday, January thirteenth 2113. Why?" the computer asks.

"Because... The last time I spoke to you was... Let me see.... It was July 26, 2000.What does that tell you?" Terrin asks the computer.

"It tells me it has been far too long, since we have had sex", she replies sarcastically, as she laughs.

"Where did you get the emotional senses at?" he asks her.

"You gave them to me. On July 27, 2000 is when you installed the laughter module and it was the next day, that you installed the emotion board. Don't you remember?" she asks him.

"No. The last time I saw you, you didn't have any of these things in you", he replies.

"Oh. I see", she says.

"Now. Can you access an outside line and tell me what is happening, outside, on the earth today?"

"Working on it. Please wait. When I get some kind of result, I will let you know", she replies as she begins trying to access an outside line.

Going up the stairs, Terrin tries to open the door. Shoving with everything he's got, it just doesn't budge. "Damn", he says as he looks for something that he can use for.... Whatever. Not finding anything in the immediate area, he goes back down the stairs and looks around the lab. "What the hell is wrong with me", he thinks to himself. "Jesus... I have a tool box", he says as he mentally kicks himself in the ass.

Going to where his toolbox always is, he opens it and finds a mini-sledge and a chisel. Taking the tools, he goes back up the stairs and starts hammering the chisel into the frame of the door. Knocking out big chunks of the door, he finally gets a small hole through it. Putting his eye up to the hole, he peers out. Not seeing anything but sunlight, he starts chiseling more of the door away.

As he gets a hole big enough to crawl through, the computer speaks up. "I have tried every way I know and cannot access any kind of phone line, or dial tone… Anywhere", the computer says. "Do you hate me?" it asks a moment later.

Looking at the computer, he starts laughing. Sitting down on the floor, he laughs till he can't laugh any more. "Excuse me, Terrin... But what is so funny?" the computer asks.

"You are", he says as he burst into a new fit of laughter.

"I...... Don't understand", the computer says.

"It's what you said.... Something I figured only a human would say... Not a computer", he replies as he starts giggling.

"Oh.... I see", the computer says as it starts making laughing noises.

Laughing at the noises coming from the computer, he thinks to himself, I need this. This is just too hilarious. "I'll be right back.... Don’t go anywhere now... You hear", Terrin asks as he starts laughing as he leaves the lab.

Going outside he sees the house is gone. Where it used to be there is now only a big hole. Looking around, he sees a few trees, but back where he came from, this place was nothing but a forest. Shaking his head, he can't believe the change this place has undergone. Looking in a southerly direction, he can almost make out, some kind of big building.

Squinting his eyes, he can almost make out a tall spire like thing, on top. Walking towards it, he doesn't see much else. No cars… No people… No animals… Nothing.... Nothing but a wasteland. What the hell happened, he wonders? Walking on, he can't believe what has happened. Yelling out, "HELLO". When no one answered, that should have told him something.

Not listening to his instincts, he plods on hoping to find someone. Maybe they could tell him what happened. Getting closer to the spire, he sees a couple of shapes near it moving around. "HEY", he yells out to them, as he waves his arms. Not making any moves towards him, he continues on. Walking for what seems like days, he finally gets to within a half mile away from the structure.

Looking up in amazement and awe, he gapes, as he looks at the thing. "My god", he says. Who or what made this he wonders. Looking around, he hasn't seen another shadow or anything since he thought he saw the first ones. Walking towards the base of the structure, he figures it is probably two miles in diameter. The top of the structure, less the spire, looked to be about six miles high. It was also probably eight miles around the middle of it.

As he gets to the base of the structure, he walks around it trying to find a door or some way of getting in. Hearing his stomach grumble from lack of food, he wishes he had something to eat right about now. Continuing to walk, he finally finds some kind of hatch, or door, or something. Looking for a switch, or lever, or maybe even a keyhole, he can't figure it out. Walking in front of it, the door opens.

Startled as the door opened, he peers in. Seeing a bunch of crates and some furniture stacked up, he sneezes as the dust starts getting disturbed. Walking in, he looks down and notices that the dust is about eight inches thick. Not believing all the dust in this place, he walks further in. When he gets about eight feet from the door, it closes, with a shwooosh sound.

Turning around as the doors close, he goes back towards them. Not opening, he gets right up next to them. Nothing. "Damn", he says looking around. Walking in the opposite direction as the door, he proceeds into the structure. Walking past furniture and cartons, piled as high as you could see, he wonders whatever happened. The sights he sees are just too unbelievable.

Shaking his head, he walks on, hoping to find something to eat, or something he can kill to eat. Looking to his left, he sees what looks like stairs going up. Walking towards them, he gets close and sees that is exactly what they are. Climbing up the steps, he stops at the next floor up and looks around. Not seeing anything worth messing with, he continues up the stairs.

As he gets near the next floor up, something comes down the stairs. Moving aside, he sees it is a head. As his gag reflexes kick in, he starts dry heaving. Trying not to think about it, he finally gets it under control. Looking up, he wants to see if someone threw it down, or if it fell by itself. Getting near the next floor, he approaches with caution. Looking closely as he climbs further up, he doesn't see anyone around.

Looking down as he gets near the top, he sees the body, the head may be from. Looking away, hoping his stomach could control itself, he starts trying to think of nice things. Looking around as he gets near the top, he steps onto the floor and walks in the opposite direction as the stairs. Not seeing any signs of life, he can't understand, what could cause such mass tragedy.

Going towards what looks like a store, or what

used to be a store. Entering the place, he looks around and sees a bunch of weapons lying on the floor. Picking up a semi-automatic Uzi, he clicks back the hammer and releases it. Putting his finger on the trigger, he holds it away from himself and fires. A short, quick burst, erupts from the gun. Startling him as it fires, he drops it on the floor. Bending down to pick it back up, a bullet just misses him by a hairs breadth.

Falling to the floor, he picks the gun up and looks around. Taking what appears to be another clip for his gun, he puts it in his pocket. Looking around in all directions, he tries to locate the source of the firing. Not seeing anything, he gets up slowly. Looking over the edge of a pile of furniture, he still can't see who, or what, was firing at him.

Standing all the way up, he starts walking towards the stairs. Just as he gets to the stairs, a shot from above just misses his left leg. Jumping back, he yells, "HEY..... YOU.... STOP FIRING".

Waiting to see if he gets a reply, the only thing he hears is the sound of more bullets, coming from above. Backing away from the stairs, he decides to investigate this floor. Maybe there's another set of stairs somewhere else, he thinks to himself, as he tries to be as quiet as he can. Looking around, he finds a regular mall. Or what used to be a mall. There were some of the structures still intact, but it looked like a lot of them were destroyed.

Entering one, he sees it used to be some kind of radio or electronics shop. Looking around at the mess, he sees some things he has never seen before. Picking them up, he looks at them and then pockets them. Not finding much of anything else, he leaves and enters the next shop. Looking up, he sees the roof, or ceiling is gone from this particular shop.

Seeing what used to be clothes or some kind of attire, he goes over and sees a nice long jacket. A duster he thinks. Trying it on, it is tight across his shoulders. Taking it back off and throwing it on the floor, he sees another one. Picking it up, he finds this one fits rather loosely. Keeping it on, he leaves and starts looking for a way up, down or out. Or just some food he thinks to himself.

Walking on, he comes to a small shop. Not seeing anything wrong with this place, he tries the door and finds it locked. Looking around he raises his foot and kicks the glass in. Reaching through, he unlocks the deadbolt. Opening the door and going in, he looks around and smiles as he sees a bicycle, that looks to be in good order.

Checking the bike out, he finds it to be in excellent shape. Carrying it out the door, he gets on and starts riding around. As he rides around, he finds a central place where it looks like all the people used to hang out at. He only knows this, because of all the dead bodies lying around. Turning away from the people, he keeps riding and looking.

Seeing what once may have been a drug store, he finds two jars of beef jerky, still in sealed containers. Opening the first one and pulling one out he unwraps the plastic and takes a bite. Chewing on it, it still has the same taste, as if it were just made. Stuffing as many into his pockets as he can, he rides on.

Looking at his watch, he sees it is 8:00 p.m. But why is it still light in here. Looking up, he still sees the bright light of outside. Hearing another gun shot from behind him, he turns around and doesn't see anyone or anything. Trying to keep the piles to his back, he rides further on into the building. Finding another stairwell, he carries his bike down the stairs.

Getting to the end of the steps, he puts the bike down and starts riding.

CHAPTER 15

Waking up next to Missy, Kensing looks over and smiles. Kissing her on the cheek, he gets out of bed and goes to the bathroom. Coming back out, he sees Missy's eyes open. Leaning up on one elbow, she asks, "So... What are we working on today?"

"I was wanting to go for a drive and take a day off from the work. I think we need a break", he replies.

"Mmmmmm... Sounds good to me", as she smiles at him.

"Cool", as he smiles back at her.

Getting out of bed, Missy goes into the bathroom and starts the water for a shower. Getting into the shower, she starts washing her body off, when she feels hands on her. Turning around, she lifts her head up and starts kissing Kensing. Kissing her back, he takes her in his arms. Making love in the shower, they finish and get their showers done.

Drying off when they get out, they go into the bedroom and get dressed. Making small talk as they get ready, he asks, "So... What are we going to take?"

"How about if we pack a small picnic and take it with us?" she asks.

"That sounds like a great idea".

When they are dressed, they go downstairs and enter the kitchen where they find a rather big mess. Getting some bread and other various things out for sandwiches, he says, "I'm going to go outside and check the truck. Make sure it has enough gas and what not", as he heads out the door.

Looking over at the lab, he sees the door standing wide open. Going over to it, he looks down inside and hears voices. Going down he sees Tabrinia and Tanya standing at a table, eating sandwiches. "Hey girls... What's up?" Kensing asks.

"Terrin.... He’s gone again. This time, it was an accident", Tanya says.

"What", he replies.

"Yeah... He was going through the doorway, when it collapsed and some of the circuits burned out", Tanya replies as she looks at Tabrinia.

"Is there anything I can do, to help?" he asks.

"Yeah... When we get the doorway open.... Would it be... You know.... Too much to ask you, to go through the doorway, when we get it working?" Tabrinia and Tanya ask at the same time.

"Hey... He's my friend. Of course I will help you. How close are you to getting it open again?".

"In about two hours. In the meantime, you can help me with the actual installation and replacement of the parts", she smiles.

"Okay... I'm pretty good at things like that".

Walking over to the pyramid, Tanya gets down on her knees and starts taking a part out. "Now, when I hand you a part... I need for you to hand me back the same part.... But a new one", as she smiles at him.

Smiling back, he says, "Okay".

Taking a part out, she hands it to him. Giving her back a new one, she installs it and works on the next one. Going through the machine in no time, they have it in good working order in three hours. "Okay... Let's try it", Tanya says.

Walking over to the control panel, she starts the sequence that starts the doorway up. Getting the sides to come down, but no light coming from it, she wonders if it is open. Sticking her hand through it, she can still see it. "Damn", she says trying to figure out what the hell the problem is.

"What?" Kensing asks.

"The actual doorway won't open", as she looks baffled by it.

"Can you fix it?" he asks.

"I might be able to... It depends on what is wrong with it", as she goes to the computer and asks it what could be wrong!

Telling her it will take a short time before an answer is available, she turns away and sits down trying to think what it could be. Looking at the pyramid, she tries her hardest to come up with an answer herself. "Have you checked the fuses?" the computer asks.

"Yeah right.... Like it's going to be that easy", she replies sarcastically.

Walking to the fuse box, she checks them all out and finds two burnt. Replacing them, she goes back to the doorway and starts it up again. When the sides come down, the green light emanates from it. "Yes", Tanya says. "Ready?" she asks Kensing.

Looking at her, he says as he shrugs, "Not really... But I said I would", as he gets ready to go through.

"Wait", Missy says as she comes down the stairs.

"What?" Kensing asks looking at her.

"You better not go anywhere without at least telling me bye", she replies.

"Oh... Sorry", as he takes her in his arms and hugs her. Kissing her as he pulls slightly away, she kisses him back.

Breaking away, he says, "Well... See you in a little bit", as he jumps through the doorway.

Getting on the other side, Kensing sees what looks like clouds... But not like clouds. The same thing Terrin saw when he went through. Walking around, he sees small specks in the distance. Walking towards them, it seems like they are moving away as he goes towards them. Running towards the things, he can't seem to get any closer.

Forgetting about them, he just walks aimlessly about as he keeps the doorway place to his back. Looking at his watch, he sees it is 12:45 a.m. Looking until his watch says 3:45, he heads back to where the doorway is supposed to be. Being careful not to get in a hurry, he takes his time walking back.

Looking around as he walks, he doesn't see anything, or anyone, except them little specks. Shaking his head, he looks up and he is back in the lab. "I didn't see anything or anyone... Well... That's not true... I saw some small specks in the distance, but the closer I got to them, the farther away they got", he relates to them.

"I don't get it", Tanya mumbles to herself.

"Hey... What if we had the computer try to duplicate exactly what happened, when Terrin went through", Tabrinia suggests.

"Let me see if it can", Tanya replies.

Going over to the computer, she asks if the computer can do that. Getting an affirmative reply, she smiles as she knows they can get her Father back. Turning the computers body sensors on, she tells Kensing to go by the computer, so it can link with his body functions. Doing as she asks, he looks at her and asks, "How will I get back, if this doesn't work?"

"We will try again, the same way, in two and a half hours... So be ready", Tanya replies.

Nodding his head, he says, "Okay... Just be sure you don't leave me there", as he smiles at her.

"Don't worry. You will get back. But don't be late getting to the door", Tanya warns.

Synchronizing his watch with the computer clock, he says, "I guess I am as ready as I will ever be".

"Okay... Computer... Start modifications

sequence three. Now engage body heat tracking... Report when ready", Tanya says.

After about five minutes, the computer replies, "Okay... Tracking system online and fully operational... All systems ready for doorway jump excelsior".

"Whenever you're ready. Go anytime and the computer will duplicate Terrin's exact movements, as close as possible. Good luck... And bring Terrin back with you", they all say in unison.

Turning around, he jumps through the doorway. As he jumps through, the same thing happened as happened with Terrin. Coming out on the other side, he sees some things flying around in the distance. Going towards them, he sees they are some kind of large creatures. Walking backwards and keeping his eyes on them, he glances over his shoulder, every now and then, to make sure nothing is behind him.

When he gets to a safe distance, he turns around and walks away from the creatures. Walking for awhile, he finally decides he is going to walk another few minutes and then head back. Looking behind him, he sees a bunch of the creatures coming towards him. Turning and running, he runs blindly. As he looks over his shoulder, he looks back around and he is just about to the control panel.

Hitting the panel at full force, he flips over it hitting the off button accidentally as he does so. Trying to catch his breath, his face turns blue, then purple. Hitting his stomach, he finally gasps as he gets his breath. Standing up when he can, he looks around and sees the lights on. "What the hell is going on here?" he asks no one in particular.

"Nothing", a soft feminine voice replies.

"Who said that?" Kensing asks as he looks around.

"I did", the computer replies.

"Who?" Kensing asks as he looks puzzled.

"The computer", it says.

"Oh.... Okay", as he wipes the sweat off his forehead.

"Is there anything you need?" it asks.

"Yeah... Where the hell is Terrin?" not expecting it to know.

"He went outside a little while ago and I haven't heard from him since", the computer replies.

"Thanks", Kensing says as he walks up the stairs.

Seeing the hole Terrin went through, Kensing crawls through it to. Coming out, it is bright as the sun shines brightly. Looking around, he sees where the house used to be. Now there's nothing but a hole. Looking down, he sees footprints leading away from the lab. Following them, he sees the structure in the distance as he gets closer.

Seeing the structure as he gets nearer, he whistles to himself. What the hell is that, he asks himself. Whatever it is, he came this way he thinks. Going toward the structure, he finally gets to it after walking for what seems like hours. Looking at his watch, he sees he is already two hours late getting back.

Shrugging his shoulders, he says, "Can't have everything... At least I know he's here".

Continuing to walk towards the massive structure, he finally gets to it. Seeing the footprints go around the thing he follows them. When he gets near the door, it opens and startles him. Looking up he sees the door. Looking inside, he sees footprints leading away from the door. Following them, he gets about six feet away and the door swooshes shut. Turning around Kensing walks back toward the door.

When he gets right next to the door, he realizes he is trapped. So is Terrin he thinks to himself. Following the footprints, he finds the stairs and the bodies that lay around every now and then. Getting past them as fast as he can, he follows the footprints until they leave the stairs. Seeing a lot of footprints all around he guesses something went wrong here. Looking around, he doesn't see anyone....... Or anything.

Going around a pile of furniture, he sees they go off away from the stairs. Following them into a store, he sees the duster he threw down. Picking it up, he tries it on. Fitting him like it was made for him, he sees the footprints going back out and away from the store. Following them he sees them go toward a small building, that looks like it is the only whole building here. Going in through the door, he notices bike treads leading away. "Damn", Kensing says out loud, without realizing it.

Following the bike tread, they stop at another store, where there are a few beef jerky's scattered about, near the front. Picking one up, he sees it is still unopened, he opens it and takes a small bite. Not bad, he thinks to himself. Eating a couple of them, he gets all that are there and puts them in his pockets.

Following the bike treads, away from the building, he looks up and sees the other set of stairs. Nodding, he sees the footprints go down. Going down, he gets to where the prints leave the stairs and follows the bike tread again. Looking at where they go, he sees a figure up ahead. Going towards it, he starts to get near.

CHAPTER 16

Riding away from the steps, he gets the eerie feeling he is being followed. Twisting his neck around, he looks behind him. Not seeing anything, he continues on. Seeing a huge pile of furniture stacked up, he also sees a hole that is big enough for him and his bike. Going into it, he watches and waits to see if, whoever, or whatever is following him, will appear.

As he watches, he starts getting tired. Looking out his eyes start closing. Falling asleep, he sleeps soundly. While he is sleeping, the shadow that was following him comes over and looks in at him. Hearing a noise, it turns around and looks back. Not seeing anything, it turns back to Terrin. Hearing something else, it turns around and Kensing stands there.

Grabbing it as it squeals, Kensing holds onto it, as tight as he can. Hearing the fight outside his hole, Terrin looks out and sees Kensing holding onto something. Getting up, he goes out and asks, "What the hell is all the noise out here. Can't anyone get some sleep? Damn... I hope you know, I have to get up and go to work tomorrow", Terrin says as him and Kensing both burst out laughing.

When Terrin says that, the thing turned its head up and looked at them. Looking at the thing, as it reveals its face, Terrin can't help it, when the thing looks familiar. It is a man, in his early thirties and he is going bald. "Do you speak English?" Kensing asks.

"Of course I do. What am I supposed to be, stupid?" he asks.

"No... No... Ummm... It's just that we were wondering, what happened? Where are all the people?"

"You mean, you don't know what happened?" the guy asks, as if it is common knowledge.

"No... We don't know what happened. We aren't.... How would you put it? Ummmmm... Not from here actually... But we are from this planet... But not really", Terrin says, (as if life weren't already confusing enough).

"Wait a minute.... What do you mean, when you say you are not from here?" the stranger asks.

"Well... We aren't", Terrin starts.

"From this time", Kensing finishes for him.

"So... You're trying to tell me you are time travelers?" the guy asks.

"Well... In a way, yeah", Terrin replies.

"Wait a minute... Wait a minute", the guy says, "This is just too confusing... Here's what we'll do. First.... You tell me exactly where you are from and then I will fill in, what you need to know", the stranger says.

"Okay. Let's see", Kensing starts saying, as Terrin cuts in and answers.

"We are from the year of 2000. My lab is in a hole in the ground where I used to live... Ohhhh... I'd say about six miles away", Terrin finishes as Kensing glares at him.

Glaring back Terrin smiles and makes Kensing even more pissed off. "So... You're the one", the stranger says, as he points at Terrin.

"What?" Terrin replies with a straight face and then he starts smiling.

"You're the one that caused all this", the stranger replies, as he backs away.

Grabbing the guys arm, Kensing says, "What are you talking about?"

"Him... He's the one that caused all this.... Mess", he replies as he looks around.

Looking puzzled, Terrin asks, (the million dollar question),"How did I cause all of this?" as he spreads his arms wide indicating everything.

"Well... It's a long story... Let me start with.... It all started, in the year of 2000.A guy was doing some secret experiments, when the FBI was hot on his trail. Following him or what they thought was him, they got the wrong guy. In the meantime, this guy was still doing his experiments. When his experiments went haywire, things started happening, that changed the course of history… For all", the guy says.

"Yeah... But I'm sure there are more than just myself doing these experiments. I mean, secret stuff", Terrin says as he looks at Kensing and shrugs.

"Yeah", Kensing says as he backs Terrin up.

"No... I saw a picture of the guy.... And boy, did he look a lot like you", he replies pointing at Terrin.

"Yeah... But everyone says that about me", Terrin says.

"No... No... No... I mean, you are the guy I saw... There's not a doubt in my mind", the guy replies firmly.

"How do you know it was actually me?" Terrin asks as a bullet just misses his head and hits the guy in the chest.

Clutching his chest, the man falls limp. Terrin and Kensing both duck down and check on the guy. Feeling for a pulse, Kensing feels nothing. "I think he's dead", Kensing says.

"Fuck...... We need to find that bastard.... I... We need to find out what exactly happened, before we go back", Terrin says as he looks around.

Not seeing anything, or anyone, they both peer around the piles of furniture they are behind. Looking up, Terrin sees movement above and to the right a little bit. Waving at Kensing, he finally looks. Pointing in the direction the guy is at, he says, in a low whisper, "Up and to the right a little bit, just below the statue like bird".

Nodding as he sees the guy, he motions for Terrin to go around his side of the pile and he will work his way around the other side. Nodding yes, Terrin moves around and looks up. Not seeing the guy, he dashes across the floor and ducks behind another pile of furniture. Kensing moves around and instantly, a bullet hits the floor, just missing his foot.

Backing up, he peers around the edge. Seeing the guy, Kensing starts backing up as he looks back. Seeing a pile of crates coming up, they look like they might be out of site. Taking the chance, he jumps behind the crates. Not hearing any gunfire he peers around the far side. Not seeing the guy, he guesses the guy probably can't see him either.

Dashing across the floor, Kensing makes it about fifty feet away, behind some furniture. Looking over in the dim light, Kensing can just barely make out a shape, moving around behind the furniture. Looking up, Terrin sees the guy hanging from a rope. Smiling to himself, he points his gun at the rope and fires. Missing, Terrin curses himself. Aiming again, he misses again. "Damn... What the hell are you... A fuckin' moron?" he berates himself.

Aiming again, Terrin lines his shot up and fires. Seeing the guy look up, the rope breaks and the guy falls down. "YES", Terrin says as he balls his hand into a fist and bends his elbow, with his fist up and then pulling it down, as he says it.

Running over to the place the guy looked like he might have fallen to, he finds him. Turning away as he sees the guy, he says, "DAMN", as Kensing approaches.

"What?" Kensing asks.

"He's dead", Terrin says as he hangs his head.

Patting him on the back, Kensing says, "Hey... It was him or us... You chose us... Thanks buddy".

"Yeah right", Terrin replies as he sounds defeated.

"Terrin... Snap out of it... I said it's all right... Okay", as he shakes him lightly.

Terrin replies in a low soft voice, "You ever touch me again asshole... And that will be all she wrote", looking at him as he starts to smile.

Looking at him, Kensing smiles and they both start laughing. Sitting down on the floor, they continue laughing. Finally getting himself under control, Terrin looks around. "Hey... Where the hell did you come from, anyway?" he asks.

"The girls set the computer to duplicate what happened to you, so it would happen to me. I was supposed to be back at the doorway in two hours, but that was", as he looks at his watch, "Ohhh about nine hours ago. So, what do we do now?" he asks.

"First... We need to get out of here and back to the lab. Then, when we get there, we have to open the gate and use my remote, to change the settings, so we go back where we were", Terrin explains to Kensing. "Sound good to you?" he asks.

"Better than what I could do".

Walking towards the stairs, they get to them and go down. Getting to the bottom of the stairs, they look around and see nothing but dimmer lights and even darker corners. Watching different sides, they go along, in relative silence,(how else can you be noisy in eight inches of dust?). Not seeing or hearing anything, they make it about eighty feet into the room, when they are shot at, from about three or four different locations.

Ducking behind a small pile of furniture, Terrin looks around and tries to see where the shots are coming from. Falling to the ground as a bullet grazes his shoulder, Kensing looks around and sees if he can see anything. Not seeing anything, a bullet hits the ground between his legs. Rolling over to Terrin, he says, "I think were in deeeeeeeeeeeeep shit".

"Shhhh..... I think I can see two of them", Terrin whispers to Kensing.

Pointing up and to Kensing's left, he shows him where one is. Nodding his head, as he sees him, Terrin aims his gun and drops one. Aiming his next shot, he fires and misses. Shaking his head slightly, he aims and tries again. Firing, he sees the guy fall. Nodding his head, he looks around the crates. Seeing one more, he aims as carefully as he can and fires....... But nothing happens. All that he hears, is the click of an empty chamber. "Shit", Terrin mutters.

"What?" he asks quietly.

"Out of bullets. Now what?" Terrin whispers back.

"Hey... Did you see where the guys you killed, fell to?" he asks.

"Sort of....... One was over there", Terrin whispers as he points in the general location.

"Okay... Let's sneak over and check for his weapon... I will keep the guys firing at me and you go over", Kensing whispers.

"Okay... I'll be right back", Terrin replies in a whisper.

Dodging in and out of the piles, Kensing keeps the guys attention on him. Terrin runs over and finds one of the guys. Not seeing the weapon, he starts rummaging around looking for it. Not finding it, Terrin goes over and moves the guy. His eyes light up as he sees a nice looking, 30-30 Winchester lying on the floor. Checking the guy's pockets, Terrin finds a couple dozen rounds of ammo.

Pocketing the ammo, he stands up and takes the rifle. Going back to where they were hiding he peers around a pile of furniture and spots one of the guys. Aiming the rifle at his rope, he fires and watches as the guy drops to the floor. Ducking behind the pile, a bullet zing's by where his face was a minute ago.

Taking a deep breath, he goes around the other side of the pile. Peering around the edge, he sees the guy. Kneeling down he places the gun between some furniture. Aiming through a small hole in the pile, he fires and just misses. Watching the guy, Terrin smiles as he sees him wriggle around. Aiming and firing again, Terrin nails him in the head. Seeing him fall, Terrin gets up and looks for Kensing.

Finding him by where one of the guys fell, he sees he also has a rifle. Nodding his head as he approaches Terrin says, "Nice gun buddy", as he smiles.

Smiling, Kensing replies, "Yeah... Can you believe, some asshole left this lying around.... I walked by and it said pick me up", as he starts laughing.

Laughing himself, Terrin says, "We still have

to get the hell out of here".

"I know. So let's go", he replies as he starts walking.

"Wait.... Your going the wrong way", Terrin states as he starts to laugh.

Heading in a totally different direction, Kensing catches up and they make small talk as they look for a way out. They look for about eight hours, before Kensing walks in front of a sensor, or something, and a small door opens in the wall. Looking out Terrin crawls through and finds himself outside. When Kensing walked through, the door closed.

"I guess they wanted us gone", Terrin says.

"Yeah... What... Are we to mean for them?" Kensing replies as they start laughing once again.

"Yeah", Terrin replies in between laughs.

Walking towards where they think the lab is, they find a small water hole. Taking a small sip, Terrin nods his head in approval. As Kensing kneels down and is about to get a drink, Terrin starts making gagging, choking sounds, as he falls to the ground and grabs his throat. Kensing drops his handful of water and backs away. As he starts gagging again, Terrin starts laughing his ass off.

"You are one of the biggest assholes I have ever known", Kensing replies trying to keep a straight face when he starts laughing to.

"Gotcha", Terrin replies as he starts laughing again.

"That you did".

Drinking as much as they can, they get up and

walk towards the lab. Walking in silence, occasionally someone will make a comment or start a conversation. Just your regular, everyday, boring walk. Ho hum. Looking up, Terrin sees the sun in the same location as when he first got here. Deciding to keep his eye on it, they walk to where they see another spire, sticking up in the sky. It looked to be about two miles away.

Pointing it out to Kensing, he nods and looks intently at it. When they have been walking for about two hours, Terrin looks up and sees the sun in the exact same place as before. The sun hasn't moved. Something bad has happened and for some reason, it's my fault, he thinks to himself. What is it though, his mind still thinks, as he tries not to.

Getting next to Kensing, Terrin asks, "Have you noticed that the sun doesn't move?".

Looking up, Kensing says, "No... I haven't. Why?"

"Because.... This is my fault... That guy said it was my fault.... It's my doorway... Somehow it has changed the world", Terrin says as he looks down and starts crying silently, as they walk.

"It's not your fault. That guy was mistaken", he replies, trying to cheer him up.

Looking at him, Terrin wipes his eyes with his arm. "Thanks", Terrin says.

"Just telling you the way I see it", he says.

"I know", Terrin says.

Looking forward Terrin sees a familiar sight. Seeing the door to the ground, he says, "We're back", as he points it out.

"All right".

Going through the hole, Terrin gets downstairs. Stepping off the stairs, the computer says, "Having sex once each day, helps keep the assholes away", as it starts in on it's computer laugh.

Laughing as the computer says that, Kensing was coming through the hole when he heard and started laughing. Scratching his neck as he laughs, he comes down and asks, "Is this the computer you have, back at the...", as he motions in a way Terrin understands.

"Yeah", Terrin replies as he smiles. "Cool ain't it?"

"Cool isn't the right word for it... Hmmm... Let's see.... Awesome is more like it".

"Hello Jennifer", Terrin says.

"Hi Terrin. Are we alone?" the computer asks in a rather sexy voice.

"No... My friend Kensing is here. Kensing... This is Jennifer... Jennifer... This is Kensing", Terrin introduces them to each other formally.

"Oh. I'm sorry for my earlier behavior. It's all his fault", the computer says.

Laughing as the computer says that, Terrin replies, "That's all right. You can say whatever you want, in front of him".

"Okay. What do you need?" she asks. "Me, I hope", she adds a moment later.

Continuing to laugh Terrin says, "No. We need you to open the doorway and make the mistake that got me here. Can you do that?" Terrin asks.

"That will take a few minutes. Hold on please", the computer replies.

Looking around Kensing sees a couple of

small computer boards lying on top of a book. Picking them up, he puts them in his pocket. Looking at the book, he reads 'Micro-Magnetic Engineering'. "Hey, have you read this yet?" Kensing asks.

"What is it?" Terrin replies.

"It's called, 'Micro-Magnetic Engineering'", Kensing says.

"No. I never knew it was written", Terrin replies.

"Well.... I guess it was", Kensing says putting the book down.

Just then, the computer says, "Anytime your ready, tell me to start and we will begin".

"Okay. Wait a minute", Terrin says as he turns to Kensing. "Ready?" as he raises his eyebrows.

"As ready as I will ever be", Kensing replies.

"Okay. Go", Terrin says to the computer, as they wait for the doorway to open. As the system starts powering up, it starts making a high-pitched whine.

As the noise becomes unbearable, it stops and you can hear the generator chugging, trying to stay on. It chugs one last time and then, everything gets dark. "Oh shit. The generator must've run out of gas", Terrin says as he stands up.

Feeling in front of him, his eyes get adjusted to the darkness. Looking towards the door, he sees the sun shining through. Seeing the lab in dim light, he can make out certain things. Heading for the door to the generator, he gets to it and opens it. As he opens it, a cloud of smoke comes rolling out. Coughing as his lungs fill up with smoke, Terrin moves back.

"Hello", Kensing says. "Damn... What was that?" he asks.

"The damn generator decided to run out of gas".

"Oh man..... Now what are we going to do?" Kensing complains.

"We need to find something we can use as gas..... Or something that would work, for maybe... Ten minutes", Terrin says.

"Let me think..... You got any alcohol?"

"I don't know. Look over the table with the cage on it, in the cabinet. I used to keep it there", Terrin says.

"Okay", he replies as he goes over and opens the cabinet.

As he opens the cabinet, a rather extra-large spider comes falling out. Jumping back as he lets out a little scream, he shivers. "What?" Terrin asks.

"A big fuckin spider", Kensing says.

"Where?" he asks.

"There", Kensing says pointing at it.

Looking at it, Terrin smiles and laughs. "Gotcha", as he laughs.

"You mean... You..." Kensing starts to say, as he throws a rag at Terrin and they both start laughing.

Laughing even harder as Kensing goes near the spider, Terrin says, "No... No... Get back. It's real".

"You asshole", Kensing says, backing away from the spider.

"Can't help it.... I have hung around people

like you... What the hell do you expect me to be?" Terrin replies as he laughs some more.

"Fuck you... Now get me something to use to smash it with," he says as he keeps his eye on the spider.

Seeing a small box that is heavy Terrin asks, "How about this?"

Looking at what he is talking about, Kensing turns back around and sees the spider gone. "Damn, I don't think we are going to need that. It's gone", he says as he looks down.

"Find it", Terrin replies.

"I'm trying to", Kensing says as he looks under things.

Taking the box over to him, he says, "When you get done playing with your friends, let me know", as he smiles.

"Right", he replies in a sarcastic manner.

Kneeling down, Terrin looks under the tables and sees the little bastard. "Right there", he says as he points.

"Where?" Kensing asks.

"In front of you and to the left", Terrin replies.

Looking where Terrin is talking about, Kensing finds the spider and drops the box. Smashing the spider, as the box falls on it, it makes a nasty mess. Plugging his nose as he gets a whiff of the smell, he starts gagging. "Damn.... That's nasty", Terrin says, as he heads for the door.

Following him, they both go back outside. Breathing in fresh air, Terrin starts laughing as the situation hits him just right as being funny. Catching his breath, Kensing says, "Man... That's worse than your farts", as he starts

laughing.

"My ass... More like yours", Terrin replies as he starts laughing.

"Eat me", he says as he sits down.

Sitting down next to him, Terrin pats him on the back and says, "Don't worry... Just cause your farts smell bad, don't mean I won't be your friend", as he starts laughing.

Pushing him over, Kensing says, "Go to hell".

"I've been there, but they were scared I was going to take over, so they kicked me out", Terrin replies in a smart-ass tone of voice.

"And here I thought you ran like a girl", Kensing says as he starts laughing.

As they both sit there and breath clean, fresh air, Terrin gets up and goes over to the door. Putting his head down into the door, he takes a small smell. Not smelling the odor anymore, he goes down. Seeing Terrin go into the door, Kensing gets up and follows him. Getting downstairs, Terrin goes to the cabinet and opens it. Looking in, he sees three bottles of alcohol. Taking one from the cabinet, he sees it is only about three-fourths of the way full.

Looking at the other bottles, he sees they also have just about as much in them. Thinking, Oh well, he takes them all and gives them to Kensing when he gets downstairs. Taking the bottles from Terrin, Kensing says, "We have to be fast. When this is being used, it will burn the generator up. It will also last about ten minutes, or about there, before it is gone. Hopefully, long enough to open the doorway up and go through", Kensing says.

"Okay... I will get the program to run as fast as I can", Terrin replies as he goes over to the computer and waits for Kensing to get the generator started.

Kensing pours the alcohol in and screws the cap on. Grabbing the pull cord, Kensing rips it. Not starting, Kensing pulls again. Chugging slowly, it starts gaining momentum as the lights come back on. Getting the computer up and running, Terrin tells it to run the program, to open the doorway. Starting the system up, the computer tells him, "Whenever your ready".

"Let's go", Terrin says to Kensing.

Going to where Terrin is he says, "C'mon... Let's go".

"All right... Now Jennifer", Terrin says as he grabs Kensing's arm and leads him to the doorway.

Jumping through, they are attacked by the flying things. Raising his rifle up, Terrin fires and takes one out. Firing with him, they soon have all the creatures killed. "C'mon", Terrin says as he starts running to where he thinks the doorway is.

Pulling the remote out of his pocket, he starts checking for doorways. Finding one, he looks at where the other one was and shakes his head sideways. Continuing on, they soon have been running for about twenty minutes. Coming to a stop, Terrin bends over, as cramps hit him. Coming up, Kensing does the same thing. "Damn.... I'm not used to that", Terrin says.

"Why did you pass the other door up for?", Kensing asks in between gasps.

"It wasn't the right one", Terrin replies, as he

starts catching his breath.

"Oh.... I didn't think it mattered", Kensing replies.

"I'm not sure if it does.... But to be on the safe side, I would rather try the same door".

"Okay... I think I understand".

Looking around, they don't see any more of those creatures. Walking the way they were going, Terrin uses the remote to see if the doorway is even close. Not seeing anything, they walk on. Reaching into his pocket, Terrin pulls out a couple of beef jerky strips. Handing one to Kensing, they open them and start eating.

CHAPTER 17

By the time they get done with them, Terrin tries the remote again. Seeing a doorway up ahead, he opens the doorway. Stepping through, they find themselves back in the right lab. Looking up as they come through, the girls run to them and hug them. "We thought you would never come back, after you didn't come back after two hours", Missy says as she hugs Kensing.

Hugging Terrin, Tanya and Tabrinia both have smiles on their faces. "I'm glad you came back", they both say in unison.

"So am I", he says. "But.... We have something to tell you", he adds.

"What?" they ask.

"Well..... The place we went to was... Well..... In the future. Once there, we found out that I am the reason for the world to come to an end", Terrin says as he lowers his head.

"Terrin... We don't know it was you", Kensing says.

"The guy said it was my fault", he replies.

"He didn't know what he was talking about".

"That's bull and you know it", as Terrin starts getting upset.

"Stop it", Tabrinia says. "Let's talk about this rationally", she adds.

"Okay", Terrin says.

"Okay", Kensing replies.

"Now... What happened?" she asks.

Telling her what they saw and what the guy said, they try to tell Terrin the guy could have been mistaken. Talking him into not thinking it was himself, they all go up to the house and head for the bedrooms. Sleeping soundly through the night, they all get up around noon, the next day. As they all wake up, the girls go downstairs to get breakfast and coffee ready. Trying to wake up all the way, Terrin gets out of bed and uses the bathroom.

Running into Kensing, as he starts heading to the kitchen, they say good morning and go in. Sitting down at the dining table, they wait for the girls to get them some coffee. As they sit there, Terrin and Kensing talk quietly among themselves. "So... What are you up to, downstairs?" he asks Kensing.

"Just trying to come up with an antidote for the patch", he replies.

"Oh... Yeah", Terrin replies, with a hint of anger in his voice.

"What's that supposed to mean?" Kensing asks.

"Nothing.... I'm sorry... I forget some things, sometimes", Terrin replies.

"That's all right", Kensing says as he yawns.

"Hey... Quit that... We just woke up and you're already, (As he yawns), tired again?" Terrin says.

"Obliviously, you are to", Kensing replies as he starts laughing.

"Go to hell", Terrin responds as they start laughing.

"What's so funny in here? Don't you guys know, you can't laugh before breakfast?" Tabrinia tells them as she brings their coffee in.

"Since when?" Terrin asks as he takes the cup.

"Since now", she replies as she smiles at him.

"Oh... Okay", Terrin says as he grabs her and pulls her closer.

As their faces get closer, Terrin kisses her. Letting her go, she goes back to the kitchen. Patting her on the ass as she walks away, she turns around and smiles. Smiling back he returns to what him and Kensing were talking about. Talking, they don't realize how much time has passed. Looking up Terrin sees the girls come in with breakfast. Setting the plates down in front of the guys, they all eat breakfast.

When they finish, Terrin and Tabrinia go to the bathroom and take a shower. Kensing and Missy go downstairs and start on their experiment. Tanya stays in the kitchen and cleans up. When she has the kitchen clean, Terrin and Tabrinia come into the kitchen and ask Tanya, if she's ready for a trip to the waterfall. Shaking her head up and down, she goes to get her things ready.

Going downstairs, Terrin asks Kensing and Missy if they would like to go. Agreeing, they all go upstairs and get their things ready. Telling Tabrinia that they are going, she smiles and says, "That's fine".

"I know. I just thought we could have a little fun, before getting back to work", he replies.

"I think it will be fun", she says as she smiles.

Just then, everyone comes into the kitchen with what they are taking. Leaving the house, they lock up and get into the truck. Driving to the spot they were at before, everyone says how beautiful it is. As they agree, they all get their tents and camp set up. Getting done, Terrin takes his pants off and then his shirt. Jumping into the water, he swims across to the other side.

"C'MON", he yells to them as he waves.

Diving into the water, Kensing swims across, to where Terrin is. The girls jump in and swim over too. Swimming over to the waterfall, Kensing says, "Hey, Terrin..... Look at these stains... Is this where?" as he starts laughing.

Giving him the bird, Terrin mumbles something, Kensing can't hear. "What was that?" he asks as he starts laughing again.

"Nothing", Terrin says as he starts laughing too.

Swimming around and joking with each other, they are all soon laughing and having a great time. As the evening wears on, they all gather around the fire and roast marshmallows. Telling ghost stories around the fire, they are soon laughing as they tell some pretty outrageous stories. When everyone starts yawning, Terrin gets up and jumps into the pond.

Swimming across to the other side, he swims

to the waterfall and sits under it, looking up at the stars. Smiling, Tabrinia dives in and swims across to him. Looking at them, Kensing sees them talking and laughing. "Hey Missy..... Let's." as he nods his head, towards the tent.

Smiling, she shakes her head up and down. Getting up, they go to their tent and zip the door closed. Tanya looks around and then decides to go for a walk. Talking and petting each other while under the waterfall, Terrin and Tabrinia are soon in an embrace. Kissing each other, they are soon naked and making love under the waterfall.

Looking over, they don't see anyone around. Resting as they get done, they lay back and snuggle together. Closing his eyes, Terrin falls asleep with Tabrinia lying across his arm. Falling asleep herself, she rolls over and puts her arm across his chest. Sleeping soundly, they forget where they are. Coming back from her walk, Tanya figures everyone must be in bed sleeping.

Getting into her bathing suit, she jumps into the water and swims around. Thinking about her mother, she can't help but cry. Why did you have to take my mother? she asks quietly as she looks up at the sky. Not getting an answer, she just sits and thinks about her life. Hearing a noise, she looks down at the water and sees her father.

"What's wrong?" he asks with a serious look on his face.

"Nothing really... Just thinking about mother".

"I'm sorry you had to see that", looking serious as if he truly means it.

"I know... It's just that", as she starts sobbing openly.

Sitting next to her, he takes her in his arms and tries to comfort her. "Everything will turn out all right", he says as he hugs her.

Hugging him back, she says, "I hope so".

"It will. I can feel it... Things are going to get better", Terrin tells her as he hugs his daughter tightly, as if he never wanted to let go.

Hugging him back just as tightly, she says, "I love you soooo much dad".

"I love you too babe. I never have, or never will, stop loving you", he replies as his eyes start to water.

"Oh daddy", she cries into his shirt.

As they sit there and hug and cry, they soon fall back and go to sleep. Sleeping soundly, Terrin all of a sudden jerks awake as he is dragged into the water. Shaking his head, he looks around and sees Tabrinia, swimming away. Swimming towards her, he starts gaining on her. Looking back, she starts laughing.

Getting within twenty feet of her, he asks, "What was that for? (Smiling slyly). Are we jealous?" as he starts back pedaling, away from her and laughing.

Jumping in, she swims after him. "I'll get you and when I do..." as she shakes her fist at him.

With all the racket Terrin and Tabrinia are making, they wake everyone else up. Coming out of their tent, Kensing asks, "What in the hell is going on?" as he rubs his eyes.

"Nothing", Terrin says as he runs by laughing.

"Hey..." as he raises his arms, trying to stop

him.

Turning around, Tabrinia bumps into him knocking him on his ass. "OOOOPS... SORRY", she yells at him as she runs away.

"What is it babe?" Missy asks as she comes out of the tent.

"It's Terrin and Tabrinia. I think they are crazy as..... As.... As a couple of bedbugs", he replies.

"Oh... Come back to bed... Come on Baby", Missy says as she starts laughing and runs into the tent.

Chasing after her, he goes in and they start kissing. Making love with the flap wide open, they are soon in the throes of ecstasy. Moaning as they have their orgasms, they soon fall asleep. Jumping in the water and heading towards the waterfall, Terrin looks back and really starts laughing.

"What the hell is so damn funny?" Tabrinia asks.

Looking at her, Tanya replies sarcastically, "Well for one... This isn't a nudist camp", as she starts laughing too.

"To hell with both of you", Tabrinia replies as she stomps off towards the tent.

"Do you think she'll stay mad at you?" Tanya asks looking at him.

"Nah", as he shakes his head, "she'll get over it", smiling slightly.

"We all do", Tanya replies.

"Ready for some coffee?" he asks.

"Yeah... Don't mind if I do", as she jumps into the water and swims across the pond to the camp.

Following her, Terrin dives in and is soon abreast of her. Looking at her, he strokes harder as he passes her up. Swimming like a champion swimmer, (even at 33), he soon reaches the other shore and looks back. "What took you sooooooo long?" he asks.

"Nothing", as she heads for the coffee stuff.

Following after her he says, "Tanya, baby... I was just kidding", he pleads.

"I know.... So was I", she replies nonchalantly.

Laughing as they get the coffee going, after getting a fire started, they are soon laughing and drinking coffee. Looking up, they see Tabrinia coming over. Just looking at her and not saying anything, she asks, "What?"

"Nothing", they say as Terrin shakes his head.

"Then why are you staring at me?"

"We weren't. We were ahhh...... Ummmmm", he falters.

"We were just glancing... But for a long time", Tanya replies as Terrin and her start laughing.

"You are both the same", Tabrinia says as she starts laughing with them.

"Now what the hell is it?" Kensing asks as he comes out of the tent.

"Nothing buddy.... It’s time for coffee. It's a new day and there are fish out there somewhere", Terrin replies.

"Oh shit... I forgot", Kensing says as he starts smiling as they both start laughing.

"You are all crazier than hootowls", Tabrinia replies as she starts laughing.

"I guess you are to. I mean, you hang out with us", Terrin replies as they all start laughing.

While the girls get breakfast ready, Terrin and Kensing get their fishing stuff out of the truck. Getting their rods set up, they cast them out and leave them. Looking towards the girls, Kensing sees that breakfast is ready. Getting up, he says, "Breakfast buddy".

"Oh... okay", Terrin replies as he gets up too.

Going towards the girls, they get there and sit down. When the girls bring their plates to them, they thank them and start eating. Glancing over at the poles, Terrin sees Kensing's rod starting to head out to the water, "Ummmmm... Kensing... Your pole man", he says as he points.

"Oh shit", Kensing says as he gets up and runs to his fishing pole.

Reeling it in, he pulls in a big rubber boot. Looking behind him, he sees them all laughing at him. Giving them the finger, he mouths the same words. Turning back around, he gets the boot unhooked and resets his hook. Casting it back out, he leaves it there while he goes up and finishes breakfast.

Getting up to go fishing, Terrin and Kensing kiss the girls bye and head for their poles. While the guys fish, the girls talk and laugh. As the day wears on, they all get tired and decide to head back early. Leaving and going back to the house, they arrive and go inside. They all head for their own rooms. Terrin and Tabrinia fall asleep the moment their heads hit the pillows. Same with Kensing and Missy.

Not being able to sleep, Tanya goes downstairs and turns the radio on. Listening to some music, she falls asleep on the floor near the fireplace.

CHAPTER 18

Waking up the next morning, Terrin smells coffee and food cooking. Mmmm, he thinks to himself. Getting up, he heads into the kitchen. Going in, he sees Tabrinia, Missy and Tanya getting everything ready. Smiling as he approaches Tabrinia, he wraps his arms around her and whispers, "Good morning babe".

Whispering the same back to him, she gets a cup of coffee ready. Handing him the cup he takes it and goes to the table. Sitting down, Kensing enters the kitchen yawning. "Hi y'all", he says to everyone, as he gets a cup of coffee and sits down, across from Terrin.

"Mornin' buddy", Terrin says as he sips his coffee.

"So... What's up your sleeves this time?" Kensing asks him as he raises his eyebrows.

"What are you implying?" Terrin asks with a serious look on his face.

"Exactly how you think I am implying it", Kensing retorts as he looks dead serious himself.

"Well... Suppose I took it as a compliment... What the hell would you do then?" Terrin replies smartly.

"I would.... I would... Kiss it", he replies as they start laughing.

"Bare it, sweet cheeks", Terrin replies as he laughs louder.

"Up yours", Kensing says back.

Bringing the breakfast in, the girls set everything up. Sitting down at the table, they all start eating. Making small talk, about who was doing what today and where. They are soon done with breakfast and going their separate ways as the girls clean the kitchen up. Going downstairs to his lab, Kensing does a few more secret tests of his own. Getting done what he needed, he sets the paste up for the gelling time.

Putting it away, he starts running regular tests on the other projects. Coming down the stairs, Missy asks, "So... What do we do now that you have the results?"

"Let's start trying a small sample and see if it works", Kensing replies.

Making a small batch of the mixture, Missy mixes it with the original formula. Taking some samples to the microscope, she looks at them. Nodding her head in approval, she shows Kensing what the results were and he smiles and nods his head. "Great... Now let's get some patches made, so we can get off this drug".

"Okay... It will probably take a couple of hours, but I think we can have them by dinner time", Missy says as she gets busy.

"That will be fine", he replies as he goes to his

special cabinet and checks his project.

Getting a small sample of the mixture, he takes it over to the microscope and checks it out. Yes, he whispers to himself. Going back to the cabinet, he takes his formula out and starts processing it into patch quality drugs. Looking over at Kensing, Missy sees he is making a batch of patches also. "What are those for?" she asks.

"Something I have been working on. Nothing to worry about", Kensing replies as he continues with his project.

Shaking her head she goes back to what she was doing. Getting enough of the mixture for six patches, she starts putting them together. Getting eight patches from his secret project, Kensing assembles them. They both have their patches ready for the final stage as they turn to put them into the patch sealing machine. Letting Missy go first, Kensing turns around and places his on the table behind him.

"So... What will those do?" she asks.

"Nothing. It's my baby", he replies.

"Well... What does it do?"

"It doesn't matter", Kensing says.

"Whatever", she says as she turns away and starts putting things away.

When she puts the last beaker away, the machine dings. Going to the machine, she takes the patches out and preps them for use. Going over, Kensing puts his patches in the machine and turns it on. Turning away, he goes back and starts cleaning up his part of the lab. Turning around, Missy sees a small drop of his secret experiment on the floor. Bending down, she scrapes it up with a pen.

Standing up, she keeps cleaning as she sets the pen on the table. Getting all the patches done, she hears the machine ding again. Smiling to herself, she finishes her patches and says, "They're done. Take your pick", she says as she offers him the tray.

Picking one up, he slaps it on. Shaking slightly as the drug takes effect, he shivers one last time and says, "Well... At least it doesn't make you scream".

Taking one herself, Missy puts the patch on and does the same thing. Taking one upstairs, she looks for Tabrinia. When Missy left, Kensing saw the pen with some stuff on it. Taking it over to the microscope, he sees it is his secret experiment. Wiping it off he puts it back with some other stuff on it.

When the patches were done, Kensing started getting them prepped for use. Finishing the patches, he puts them in a secret place. Turning around as Missy comes back down the steps she says, "We have one left. I am going to put it in the fridge", as she goes over and puts it away.

"Well... Now what do we do?" she asks.

"I don't know", Kensing replies with a blank expression on his face.

"What do you mean you don't know?" she asks.

"Well.... We did what we wanted to do..... We could go see if Terrin needs help with his project?" he asks.

"Okay... It's something", as she heads to the

stairs.

Following her, they go upstairs and head out to the lab.

Leaving the table, Terrin went out to the lab and started checking some things out. Running some figures through Jennifer, his computer, he finds a few different flaws, from the Colorado project. "Damn", he mutters. Going up the stairs he heads for the tree, where the satellite dishes are and he starts climbing up. Getting to the top, he starts readjusting the dishes, to what the computer specified.

Taking a small object out of his pocket, he puts it in the center of the dish. Checking the readings displayed on it, he nods, as the first one is fine. Checking the others, he readjusts them, as they are not where the computer specified. Getting them pointing to the right coordinates, he climbs back down. Going back down to the lab, he checks them with the computer and sees they are within specs.

Powering the system up, he opens the doorway. Feeling leery about going in, he turns the system off and decides to wait for someone else to get here. Getting things cleaned up, he is recalibrating his remote, when Tabrinia and Tanya come down. "Hi babe", Tabrinia says as she comes down.

"Hi dad. Need some help?" Tanya asks.

"Yeah.... As a matter of fact... I do", he replies as he smiles at them. "C'mon. Here's what I need", as he explains to them what he is trying to do.

Shaking their heads in understanding, they get busy getting all the stuff done. "Oh shit", Terrin says as he remembers the safety the other computer setup had.

"What?" Tabrinia asks.

"Oh... It was something I had forgotten about. I am going to integrate a safety in the system. You know.... So we can power the system up, but the actual doorway won't open till we want it to", he says refreshing her memory.

"Oh yeah", she replies as she remembers him telling her.

Going over to the computer, he starts making a program, so he can delay the doorway manually. Taking most of the afternoon to get all his things done that he needed done, he looks at his watch and sees it is 6:45 p.m. Shaking his head he says, "I think it's time we went up to the house and relaxed for awhile. We can finish tomorrow".

They both agree, as they head up the stairs and lock up. Getting to the top, Terrin sees Kensing and Missy coming over. "Hey... What's up dude?" he asks.

"Not a lot. We were just coming out, to see if you needed any help?" Kensing replies.

"We are going to finish tomorrow. It's time for dinner and relaxation", he says.

"Sounds good to me", Kensing says as he turns back around.

"We'll be in… In a minute", Terrin says as he helps the girls out.

Closing and locking the doors, they all go into the house. As the girls go into the kitchen and get dinner ready, Terrin finds Kensing sitting on the front porch. Going out Terrin asks, "So... How's your project coming?"

"We finished it. That's why we were coming out to help you", Kensing replies as he looks at him.

Looking at Kensing he says, "That's cool. So.... What was it?" Terrin asks.

"A drug that gives you ESP abilities. Things like that. But it had a drawback.... It was addictive. So now we have a cure for that, without losing the abilities that you got from the drug", he explains.

Nodding his head as he seems to understand, Terrin says, "Cool".

"Yeah.... I thought so too", Kensing replies.

Sitting back, they look out at the skyline and remember what the other place was like. "Well.... At least we don't see the tower poking up into the sky", Terrin says.

"I hear that", Kensing replies. "So... That's what the future looks like, huh", he adds.

"Yeah... I guess so", Terrin replies. "Although I wouldn't want to live there", as he lights up a cigar.

"Yeah... Me either. I couldn't stand no one else around".

Poking her head out the door Tanya says, "Dinner's ready".

"Okay", they both say in unison.

Getting up, they walk into the house and sit down for dinner. Waiting for the girls to get the rest of the food in, they talk about what they need to do the next day. Finishing their conversation, the girls bring the rest of the food. Sitting down at the table with the guys, they dig in and eat. As they all finish their meal, the girls clear the table and tell the guys to wait a minute. Sitting at the table, they wait. About five minutes later the girls come in with the most beautiful cake ever.

It was a pyramid, with brown and gray frosting. There was a needle sticking out of it, with Kensing spelled out on it. Looking closer Terrin sees his name there, on the pyramid. The needle was done with black, white and red. "That is so cool", Terrin says as he stares at the cake.

"I second his opinion", Kensing says as he gapes at the cake.

"Thanks girls.... You are definitely the best ever", Terrin replies as he smiles from ear to ear.

"Yeah... Thanks", Kensing says as well.

"Well... We figured with what you guys have been doing with us, this is the least we could do in your honor", they all say in unison, as they smile.

Hugging the girls, after they set the cake down, they all get their hugs and kisses out of the way. Grabbing the knife, Terrin is just about to cut it, when Kensing grabs his hand with the knife. Looking at him, they both start laughing as they cut the cake. Slicing it up a few times, they serve the cake. Giving everyone the same size piece, they are soon so full they feel they are going to explode.

Waving his hands to ward the girls off, Terrin says, "No more.... That's all the niceness my body and mind can take", as he bursts out

laughing.

Cracking up laughing as Terrin says that, Kensing can't help himself. Pretty soon, everyone is laughing and they are having a great time, (But not for long. Their fun is about to end very abruptly. For very soon, I am going to really stick it to them, HAHAAHAHAHA). Laughing and joking around for about forty-five minutes, Terrin says he needs to get some work done.

Heading for the door, Kensing asks, "Need some help?"

"Sure. C'mon", Terrin says as he motions with his hand.

CHAPTER 19

Following Terrin down to the lab, they are soon enrapt in his doorway. Reworking the calculations, Terrin asks Jennifer, (the computer, in case you skip through books), if she can recheck all her data banks, to be sure of the information. Complying, she says it will take about two hours. Nodding his head, he starts the doorway up.

"Hey, Kensing. Watch this", Terrin says as he turns a knob.

Watching the pyramid, he sees little lights flickering about. "That's cool as hell", Kensing says.

"I just happened to be messing around one day, when I came upon this. I think its neat. I have sat in here for hours at times and just watched them", Terrin confesses.

"I think I would too", as he smiles as he looks at it's beauty.

Showing Kensing some of the basics of his machine, Kensing fesses up and tells him about his little experiment. Talking about their little experiments, they are soon laughing and really getting into just having a great friendship again, (Some people would call it male bonding). As the time goes on and they talk, Jennifer says, "New data in. There were sixteen errors in the configurations".

"I thought there were a few errors somewhere. Jennifer... Print the new changes and then run Diagnostic six, level three......... Plus the anti-virus program", Terrin says as he goes over to the printer.

Waiting for Jennifer to print the new pages out, Kensing walks over and says, "So... Computers do make errors".

"Hell yeah they do. I think some of them make mistakes on purpose", he tries to whisper to Kensing.

"I heard that", Jennifer says as the document prints out.

"I'm sorry Jennifer", Terrin replies. "It won't happen again".

"Apology accepted. Running Diagnostics", as a message runs across the screen... System is temporarily down... Please wait.

Looking at the sheet Terrin says, "Yes... I thought so... Damn.... I was right", he says obliviously elated.

"What... What?" Kensing asks.

"I thought the settings were different than the Colorado test. I was right. The computer put a couple of figures in wrong and came up with the wrong figures", he explains.

"And..... This means... What exactly?" Kensing asks as he shakes his head.

"It means that I am going to go to the one place, the dog never wanted to come back from. Once there, I am going to check it out. Also... Once I go through the doorway... You leave it running. I will turn it off and on with my remote. I need you to sit here and tell the girls some bullshit story. In other words... Cover for me. I want to do this so bad. Can you be up and about... Ohh ..... Let's say...... At four a.m.?" Terrin asks.

Thinking about it, Kensing says, "Yeah... I guess I could... If it would help?"

"Of course it would. We are best friends, are we not? Don't we tell each other everything we wouldn't dare tell anyone else?" he asks.

"Yeah... As a matter of fact we are. And yes... We do tell each other everything", Kensing replies as he looks him in the eye.

Looking him back in the eye Terrin says, "What are you hiding Kensing?"

"Nothing", Kensing says trying not to look guilty.

"That's bullshit and you know it", Terrin says as he looks away in disgust.

"Okay... Okay... It's my experiments. I have a drug that makes you extremely powerful, with ESP talents. I mean, the power to do as you wish, at will. Think of the possibilities", as he pats him on the back.

"I can see what you're saying. You and me are just alike... Trying to make the world a better place, even though our projects can hurt others, if used wrongly. Why is that I wonder?" Terrin muses as he pats Kensing on the back.

"Hell if I know", Kensing replies.

"Diagnostics complete..... Found six errors... Fixed six errors.... All systems running at maximum performance", Jennifer says.

"Okay... Thanks Jennifer", Terrin says.

Reaching into his pocket, Kensing feels something. Pulling his hand out, he looks and sees that he is holding the modules from the other lab. "Terrin... Check these out", Kensing says as he hands them to him.

Taking the two objects Kensing hands him, he looks at them and then looks up as he says, "These are emotion and sensitivity chips. I wonder....", Terrin says as he goes over to the computer.

Taking the cover off the case, he looks around inside and says, "Aha".

"What?" Kensing asks as he watches.

"I can plug these babies right into the PCI slots. Hold on", as he turns the computer off.

Waiting for the system to shut down, he flicks the power switch as it gets done. Plugging one in, then the next one, he turns the computer on. Booting up, it finally loads up. Going in, Terrin uses the mouse and puts the Jennifer program to run at start up. Double clicking on the icon, the program starts running as it says, "Well... What do we have here? A couple of young studs, who look like they are hot enough to melt my circuits", in a rather sexy voice.

Laughing, as the computer says that, they soon stop laughing and start checking things out. Having the computer run the new tests for him, the computer prints them out. Looking at the results, he sees they are the same as the new printouts, the computer gave him before the diagnostics. Shaking his head, he looks a little closer and sees a minor figure change in these newest figures.

Inputting the new data, Terrin opens the doorway wide open. Jumping through, he sees the clouds and feels the calmest of feelings. Going back to the lab, he shuts the system down. "Okay... We are in business", Terrin says as he gives Kensing a high five.

"All right... So it's tonight... Right?" Kensing asks.

"Yeah... I want to do this so bad I can taste it", Terrin replies as he starts getting anxious.

Turning everything off, they go up the stairs and head for the house after locking up. Getting into the house, they find the girls and go bug them. Talking and laughing as they cut jokes and rag on each other, the girls soon leave and start making a snack. As Terrin and Kensing talk privately, Kensing says that while he is gone, he is going to try his new patch out. Agreeing with him, Terrin says he has to stay away from the equipment when he did it.

Nodding his head, Kensing agrees. Just then Tabrinia came in and said the snack was ready. Getting up, they go into the kitchen. Sitting down at the table, they see a fine snack. Smelling as he comes in, Terrin remarks, "Mmmmmmm..... That smells so good".

"Thanks", the girls say as they bring in the rest of the snack.

Sitting down with the guys, they are soon

embroiled in conversation and eating. Making small talk and finding out what they are all going to do the next day, they are soon laughing and having a good old time. As they finish off their snack, they sit back and reflect on the past. Remembering old times, they tell the funniest stories of their lives.

The girls get up and clean the dishes away. Going into the kitchen after getting the table cleared and wiped off, Terrin and Kensing go out onto the porch and talk. Talking about the trip they just came back from, they try to figure a way to stop whatever it is that's going to happen. "Yeah, but it could be anything that makes it happen. We just don't have enough information to figure out what that guy was talking about", Terrin says.

"I know... But we can make some guesses and maybe we can figure it out", Kensing replies.

"And you don't seem to understand. You can't change what will be. You see... If you go there and it is already made.... You can't change it. Once you get to that point..... It stays that way, no matter what anyone does" Terrin tries to explain.

"So... You're telling me, that it has to happen that way?" Kensing asks.

"Yes... We have already made sure of that", Terrin says. "Once we went there, we set in motion the fate of our planet", he adds.

"That's crap... I can't believe we did that", Kensing says as he looks down.

"It was an accident. We didn't do it on purpose. How could we have known that it would be like that?" Terrin asks.

"Okay... Yeah... I guess it was an accident", Kensing says as he starts getting some spirit again.

"I never would have done it, had I known that... But the newest figures take you elsewhere. I don't think it consists of time travel either", Terrin says as he tries to explain why he knows this.

Nodding his head in understanding, the girls come out on the porch and join them. Talking about the camp out they took, they laugh and remember when Tabrinia knocked Kensing on his ass, as they were having a great time. Yawning as the night wears on, Terrin and Tabrinia go to their bedroom and go to bed. Kensing and Missy go to bed also. Tanya sits out on the porch and just looks up at the stars.

Trying to remember what her mom was like, tears come to her eyes. 'Oh Mom... Why did this have to happen to you?" she asks herself. Crying about her mom, Tanya falls asleep sitting on the porch.

Waking up at 3:30 a.m., Terrin sneaks out and heads for the lab. Meeting Kensing in the hall, they both go to the lab. Getting downstairs, Terrin shuts the door after they get in. Going to the control panel, he turns the system on. Starting the computer up, Jennifer says, "Well, well, well... What do we have here? A couple of guys trying to be sneaky? You do know it's 3:45 a.m. don't you?"

"No... We didn't know... We just happened to wake up and decided to come down here.

What... Do we look stupid or something?" Terrin replies as they start laughing.

Laughing with them, the computer says, "Good morning, Terrin and Kensing".

"Good morning Jennifer", Terrin replies.

"Mornin' ", Kensing replies as he rubs his eyes. "Hey Ter... Is there any coffee down here?"

"Yeah... Over by the fax machine. In the cabinet underneath is the stuff", Terrin replies. "Jennifer... I need you to start the system up and give me visual figures on the monitor".

"Okay... Starting system circuits... Engaging system safeties.... Powering system up", the computer replies, as the system comes online and powers up.

Going over to the monitor, Terrin looks at the figures and then checks them with the print out from the day before. Nodding his head, he sees one minor discrepancy and changes it. Shaking his head, he says, "Okay... I'm ready as soon as I have a cup of coffee… Or two".

"I'll be ready in a few minutes", Kensing says as he sips on a cup of coffee.

Walking over to the coffeepot, Terrin gets his cup and makes a cup of coffee. Stirring it up after he puts the stuff in, he looks at the doorway and comments, "We have really come a long way, since we first met".

"That we have... Who would've ever known we would be doing what we are doing today?" Kensing replies.

"I know... It's strange. It's almost like someone else's life", Terrin remarks as he smiles.

"I know what you mean there... It's almost like a dream, where you see yourself and wonder, what you are doing?" Kensing adds.

"Yeah... That's it", Terrin says.

Finishing off his coffee, he gets one more cup. Walking back over to the computer, he rechecks the figures again. Nodding his head, he says, "In five minutes, open the doorway for twenty seconds. I need a one minute warning when you get ready and then the same warning as always, telling me when to go", Terrin says to the computer.

"Okay... Starting initiation sequence... Now. You have five minutes, before door opens", the computer says.

Walking back to the coffeepot, Terrin downs the last of his coffee and sets his cup down. Turning to face Kensing, he says, "Man, am I scared. I hope everything goes all right. Well, good luck on your patch", Terrin says as he holds his arms out, waiting for a hug.

Hugging him, Kensing says into his ear, "You too man. Have a good trip and make it back in one piece".

Breaking apart, Terrin walks to the doorway and waits. Just then, the computer says, "One minute warning... You have less than one minute... Please be ready".

"Jennifer... Set the default to stay online and triggered by remote only", Terrin says hoping he has activated the program in time.

"Program loaded. Remote control will be the master system. Fifteen seconds", the computer says.

"Well... See you", Terrin says as he checks to make sure he has his remote. Feeling it in his pocket, he gets ready to jump.

"The doorway is now open", the computer says.

Waving bye, Terrin jumps through. Getting to the other side, Terrin takes his remote out and closes the doorway. Keeping the coordinates in memory, Terrin walks away from the doorway. Walking along he is amazed at the feeling he gets, walking here. It's like he's come to terms with himself. This place is so calm and serene.

He has never felt like this before. Walking along, he sees that these cloud-like things also make small hills and mountains, in the distance. Walking towards the mountains, he is curious, as to where they go. Looking all around in amazement and awe, he just can't believe the way he feels. He is giddy, yet scared. Anxious, yet afraid. Mixed feelings.

As he walks along, it seems like the mountains are far away, yet, in only a short distance, he has covered at least ten miles, in a half-mile. Walking along, he looks for doorways anywhere near him. Not seeing anything, he continues on his journey. Looking up, he sees this mountain, going straight up. Walking around the mountain, he comes to the front of it. Looking up, he sees a very bright, white light, emanating from whatever was up there.

Backing up a little bit, he gets a slight glimpse of what is up there. When he gets his one and only glimpse, he sees a heavenly face. A familiar face. Getting scared, he starts running to the back of the chair. As he runs, he keeps looking over his shoulder to make sure the back of the chair is always behind him.

Activating his remote, he looks for the first sign of a doorway. He runs for what seems like hours. Not running out of breath, he looks over his shoulder and still sees the chair. It is only about a mile away. It has been a mile away for a few miles now. Not understanding what is happening, he just keeps running.

When Terrin jumped through the doorway, Kensing went over to where he and Terrin agreed for him to go. Taking a patch out of his pocket, he slaps it on his arm, above the sleeve. As he waits for the drug to take hold of him, he sits down on the floor. All of a sudden, he is gripped in the most terrifying pain ever. It feels like someone is slowly, cutting him wide open as they cut him, layer by layer. Screaming out in pain, he is soon writhing about the floor, in agony.

Out of the blue, the pain just stops. Shaking his head, Kensing feels great. He feels so alive. He feels so.... So.... So powerful. He feels like he can do anything. Testing his abilities, he tries to move a cup with just a thought. Taking more concentration than he thought, he eventually gets the cup to rise. Smiling, he starts testing all of his abilities.

CHAPTER 20

Feeling someone coming, he sits in a chair and pretends to be sleeping. The door opens and Tanya comes down. "Hello... Is anyone down here?" she asks.

Acting like she woke him up, Kensing says, "Yeah... What are you doing down here?" he asks her.

"I couldn't sleep and thought I heard screams coming from in here", she explains. "What are you doing down here? Does my dad know you're here?" she asks, accusatorily.

"Yeah, he does... In fact, he told me to stay here until he came back. He should be getting back in a short time".

"Can I stay and wait?" she asks.

"Sure... I don't mind".

"I'm going to start the computer up and check a few things", Tanya says.

"NO... Don't touch that. He has it set up to work with the remote only. He specifically told me, not to touch anything", Kensing says.

"Okay... Okay, don't have a cow", she replies.

"I'm not... You are", as he smiles.

"I'm sorry. I'm not used to having someone tell me what to do, except my mom", she says.

"That's all right... I understand".

Trying to run faster, he sees the chair disappearing from view. Looking ahead, he sees the doorway. When he gets near, he activates it and then jumps through. Coming through the doorway, he sees Tanya and Kensing talking and laughing. "I'm back", he says.

"So... What was it like?" Kensing asks.

"It was different.... But I have a very good idea of where it is, that it goes", Terrin says.

"Where?", Kensing and Tanya ask together.

"I can't say just yet... I will tell you in a little while.... I need some time alone, to sort my thoughts and feelings out", Terrin says. "Jennifer... Security lock down, TDA4657SIN13 lock".

"Security lock in place and active", the computer says as it shuts down the system and related machines.

Walking up the stairs, Terrin leaves the lab and takes a walk. Shaking their heads as he leaves, Kensing asks, "What the hell was that?"

"I don't know... He's never done that before", she replies.

Leaving the lab, Kensing and Tanya go into the house, looking for him. Not finding him anywhere, they start looking outside. "Damn... He's gone", Kensing says.

"I'm sure he will come back", Tanya replies.

"I don't know.... Maybe something happened

in there that changed him, or did something to him that made him..... Different", Kensing suggests.

"Don't say things like that about my Father", Tanya says in defense of Terrin.

"Hey... It was only a suggestion... I don't know", Kensing explains.

"I'm sorry... I just couldn't take losing my dad to", she explains to him as to why she is so defensive.

"I know... I'm sorry about that too".

"It's not your fault".

Going back into the house, they go their rooms and fall asleep. Leaving the lab, Terrin walks out into the woods. Trying to sort out his feelings and get his thoughts straight, he walks until he finds a nice quiet, little spot. Sitting down on a stump, he ponders what life is all about. Why he is even here? What his life is supposed to do, for mankind. As he muses over these thoughts and similar ones, he eventually falls asleep sitting against the stump.

When everyone at the house wakes up, Tabrinia starts asking if anyone knows where Terrin is. Tanya and Kensing speak up and tell her about the test run and that he left, after locking the system down" He'll be back. Don't worry", Tanya says to her as she goes over to her.

"I know... I just wish he wouldn't do things like this, though".

"That's my dad", Tanya says trying to lighten the mood up.

"Let's make breakfast and maybe he will be

back by then".

"Okay", Tanya says as they head to the kitchen.

In the middle of making breakfast, Terrin walks in the door.

Waking up as he is leaning against the stump, he arches his back, trying to get the kink out of it. Hearing it pop, he straightens up and yawns. Standing up, he starts heading back to the house. Reflecting on what he has learned and found out he decides on what he is going to tell them. Walking a little faster, he finally sees the house come into view.

Heading for the door, he walks into the kitchen as the girls are preparing breakfast. "Hello everyone", as he walks in.

"And just where in the hell have you been, mister?" Tabrinia asks in a playful tone.

"It's not where in the hell I have been, but where in heaven, I have been", he replies, smartly.

"What?" everyone asks.

"Nothing. Just a little joke", as he laughs.

"That figures", Tabrinia says as she wraps her arms around his neck and hugs him.

Hugging her back, they hug for about three minutes. Breaking apart, he gives her a quick kiss and then gets a cup of coffee. Going to the table, he sits down and waits for breakfast. Sitting down next to him, Kensing asks, "So... What was it like there?"

"I will tell everyone, as soon as I have eaten breakfast. I think the answer will astonish all of you".

"Really?" Kensing asks.

"Yeah... Really".

Bringing breakfast in, they eat and then question Terrin over what he found out. "Okay... I went into the doorway this morning.... When I got there, I saw some amazing things... I also felt like I was at peace with myself. It was weird! It was like nothing I've ever experienced before", he starts out.

"What do you mean, weird?" Tanya asks.

"Well... You know, how something doesn't quite, feel right?" he asks.

"Yeah", she says.

"Well... It's something like that, but more intense".

"Okay... Go on", Kensing says.

"Okay... I got there and walked for what seemed like hours. But I never got tired and when I walked, it was like I was walking ten miles, for every half-mile. It was odd. And then... When I got so far, I noticed this big cloud that went straight up.... When I went around it, I saw a bright light, but it didn't hurt to look at it... And that's when I saw him", he says.

"Who", they all say.

"Him", as he looks up.

"What?", they ask.

"HIM", Terrin says pointing up.

"You mean.... You saw", Tanya asks in amazement.

Nodding his head, he starts crying lightly. "What's wrong?" Tabrinia asks as she puts her arm around him.

"It's just the feeling I get, that something bad is going to happen", in between sniffles.

"It will be all right", she says consoling him.

"I hope so".

Wiping his eyes off, he looks at her and wraps his arms around her. Smiling as he looks at her, she smiles back. Getting up, they walk to their room and lay down. Snuggling with each other, they fall asleep for a short while. When Terrin and Tabrinia left, the others all talked about the possibility, that he was right.

Going over all the questions they have, they try to figure out if he is right. Saying he did have a door to hell, why not heaven too. Of course, that could be far-fetched. Trying to convince themselves that he may be crazy and that it was actually to a different hell.

CHAPTER 21

Waking up at 6:00 p.m., Terrin and Tabrinia jump into the shower, where he starts getting intimate. Touching her in the way that only he can, she starts getting turned on. Turning around, she starts kissing him. Kissing her back, they soon make love and then finish their shower. Getting out they dry off. Going into the bedroom, Terrin gets dressed in shorts and a large, loose shirt. Slipping his sandals on, he waits for Tabrinia.

Drying off, Tabrinia goes into the bedroom and sees him already dressed. Getting shorts and a short sleeve shirt, she puts some flip-flops on. Leaving the bedroom, they go into the kitchen and see that Tanya and Missy are in there making dinner. "Well... Isn't this nice", Terrin says as they come in.

"It sure is", Tabrinia agrees.

"Hi you two", Tanya and Missy say.

Walking to the table, Terrin sits down and looks at the paper sitting there. Reading the headlines, he sees something that makes him turn white. The headline reads, "Wanted;

Kensing Furman in the abduction and kidnapping of Missy Johnson. Also wanted, was Terrin Ashcrog for the theft of private property. Also for arson, for the burning of his house. If anyone has seen these fugitives, please call 555-8675 and you can be eligible for a reward for up to $10,000.00.

"Holy shit", Terrin mutters to himself.

"Nice headlines... Huh?" Kensing asks as he sits down across from him.

"Crazy. I never burned my house down. And about the stolen property... That's a bunch of bullshit", he says.

"Like mine. I never kidnapped Missy. She's here of her own free will. She can leave anytime she wants to", Kensing says.

"I think someone has it out for us. Who did you piss off?" Terrin asks him.

"It wasn't me... Maybe it's that girl in Colorado, that got pissed at you", Kensing says.

Putting his finger to his lips, he says, "Shhhh... Be quiet".

"Oh... Sorry", Kensing says.

"Dinners served", Missy says as she brings in a plate with steaks on it.

Bringing in a bowl of vegetables and another bowl with potatoes, Tanya sets them down on the table. Bringing in the plates and silverware, Tabrinia sets the table real quick. Going back into the kitchen, Missy gets some drinks for everyone. Bringing them back to the table, she sets a glass down in front of everyone.

Eating dinner and talking lightly, pretty soon everyone is asking Terrin questions, about the place he went to. Giving them the best answers he can, he explains to them why he came up with these conclusions. Agreeing with him, they finish dinner and have dessert. Getting done, they leave the dishes as they are and go into the living room.

Sitting down, they talk about the possibility. "I mean... What if we are the only ones with a doorway to GOD? Do you know what that could mean?" Kensing says.

"Wait a minute. What are you talking about?" Terrin asks.

"You know... We could be the doorway evangelists, who go around healing people for money", he says as he smiles and then starts laughing.

Laughing with him, everyone starts yawning. "Well... Till tomorrow", Terrin says as he rises and takes Tabrinia's hand.

Leading her to the bedroom, they get undressed and have some fun. Kensing and Missy also leave. Going to their bedroom, they get undressed and she notices the new patch. "Just what the hell is this?" she asks pointing at the patch.

"It's something I have been working on. Nothing for you to concern yourself with", he explains.

"Bullshit. If it's on your body, it does concern me", she replies.

Pushing him down onto the bed, she jumps on his chest and waits for an explanation. "Well.. It's just about the same thing as before... Only this one is stronger", he admits.

"I thought you said you were going to quit working on that kind of thing".

"I never said that. I said I wouldn't be so obsessed, with that particular field", as he smiles up at her.

"Oh... So now your trying to say I am hearing things", she says in an accusatory tone.

"No.... Listen babe. This is a designer kind. It will only work with my DNA and no one else's. So I don't have to worry about someone else using it".

"Yeah... But why did you continue on with it. You know how I feel about this stuff", she says pleadingly.

"I'm sorry. I will quit. This is it", he says to her.

"You promise?" she asks.

"I promise", he replies.

"Okay. Then let's not let it happen again", she says as she bends over and kisses him.

Kissing her back, they make love before going to sleep. Going into the lab down in the basement, Tanya looks around, for anything suspicious looking. Not finding anything that she can use, she opens a cabinet and finds a small dish, with some stuff in it. Taking it to the microscope, she looks at it. Shaking her head, she starts making another kind of drug, just like this one.

Turning the computer on, she finds Kensing's special notes and finds out they are designed specifically for his DNA. Finding a small sample of the old drug, she makes some more. Taking the samples of DNA she acquired, she starts making her own batch for someone else.

Finishing the whole procedure, before anyone wakes up, she holds up ten patches. Smiling to herself, she takes them upstairs and hides them in her bedroom.

Lying down on the bed, she falls asleep. Dreaming that her mother was still alive, she is happy and excited. Having a most favorable dream, she wakes up that afternoon as happy as can be. Going into the kitchen, she sees everyone packing food and drinks in a basket. "Where's everyone going?" she asks.

"Oh... Were going to have a picnic in heaven", Tabrinia says.

"What?" she says astounded.

"I said, we were going to have a picnic, in heaven. What more can you ask for?" Tabrinia says.

"You're all crazy", Tanya remarks. "I can't believe you people", as she stomps out of the kitchen.

Chasing after her, Terrin explains that they are only going because it is so calm and serene. It will help us all to relax a little more. Why don't you come with us and see for yourself", he suggests.

Looking at him, she asks, "Really?"

"Yes... It will be good for you", as he sounds somewhat convincing.

"Well.... Okay", she says as she joins them in the kitchen.

Going into the bathroom, Kensing pulls the one patch off and replaces it with another one. As it takes effect, he squelches the pain, so no one hears. Squeezing his gut, he finally is over the spasm. Flushing the toilet, he turns the water on and washes his hands. Coming out of the bathroom, he goes back into the kitchen. "Well... What are we waiting for?" he asks.

"Nothing... Let's go", Terrin says sounding like an amusement park attendant.

Going to the lab outside they go down. Going over to the computer, he starts the system up and enters his password. Coming online the computer asks, "So... What do a condom and a whore have in common?"

Not getting any response the computer says, "And the answer is, they both take money to use them", as you hear a computer simulated laugh.

"Don't mind her. She can get to be a little outlandish at times", Terrin says. "Jennifer, open the doorway and enter the security codes. I also want total remote capabilities. Activate..... Now", he adds.

The doorway opens and they all enter it. Pulling the remote out of his pocket, he closes the doorway. "Well.... What do you think?" he asks spreading his arms wide.

"This is so cool", Kensing replies.

"Awesome", Tanya says as she looks in amazement.

"This is by far, the best place in the world", Tabrinia and Missy say together.

Getting everything set up, they are soon talking and laughing. Eating lunch and talking about good times, they are soon in the middle of a battle. Feeling small stones come raining down around them, they get up and get ready to leave. Opening the doorway, they all go through and back into the lab.

Closing the doorway, Terrin says, "It didn't do that, when I was there".

"That was too weird. I think he knows about us", Tanya says.

"I don't know. I think maybe we should shut everything down and start again tomorrow", Terrin suggests.

They all agree. Turning the system off, he turns the lights off as he leaves and locks the doors. Going back to the house, they all go to the living room and discuss what just happened. As their discussion turns into an argument, they all go to bed, pissed at each other. Waking up at midnight, Terrin goes to the bathroom. Hearing a sound from downstairs, he goes investigates.

Entering the living room, he doesn't see anything. Going into the kitchen, he sees a light under the basement door. Opening the door slowly, he sneaks downstairs and watches, as Kensing puts two more patches on. When Kensing turns his head to look at something near Terrin's location, he sees a glazed over look in them. More like a crazy look.

Shaking his head, he starts back upstairs. As his foot hits a marble, laying on the step, it makes a noise as it hits a pan. Leaping up the stairs, Terrin jumps out the door and closes it as fast as he can. Slowly closing it the last inch, he sneaks away and back to bed. Hearing the door open as he goes to his room, he opens his door slowly and goes in.

Closing it just as quietly, he goes over and gets into bed. Snuggling with Tabrinia he closes his eyes, as someone opens the door and then closes it. Damn that was close, he thinks to himself. Closing his eyes, he falls asleep. Waking up as Tabrinia gets out of bed, he says, "Good Mornin' ".

"Good morning to you to", she smiles at him. "Join me for a shower", as she smiles slyly.

"Sure", he says as he crawls out of bed and smiles devilishly himself.

Going into the bathroom, they get into the shower and make love, while they shower. Getting out and drying off, they both go into the bedroom and get dressed. Going into the kitchen, they start making breakfast. In the middle of making breakfast Tanya and Missy enter. Missy asks as she comes in, "Has anyone seen Kensing?"

Shaking their heads no, she gets a frustrated look on her face. Going outside, she looks for him. Leaving Tabrinia and Tanya to finish breakfast, Terrin goes out and helps Missy. "Have you looked in the basement?" he asks.

"No", she says as she shakes her head.

"Okay... Let's start their then", Terrin suggests.

Going into the kitchen, they go down into the basement. "Kensing... You here?" Terrin asks.

"Go away. Leave me the hell alone", he replies.

"Kensing... It's me Missy... What's wrong babe?".

"Nothing.... Just leave me alone", he repeats.

Looking around, Terrin sees him. Going over to him, he puts his hand upon Kensing's shoulder. As his hand touches his shoulder, he turns his face around and Terrin sees a crazier look on his face, than he has ever seen before. As Kensing opens his mouth to breathe, Terrin gets a whiff of something that should have been dead. "I SAID.... LEAVE ME THE FUCK ALONE", as he grabs Terrin by the throat and picks him up.

Throwing him across the room, Terrin lands in a heap. Shaking his head, he tries to stand up and falls over. Breathing in, he looks up and sees Kensing coming after him. Trying to stand up, Terrin holds onto a small table and stands. Reaching his arm out, Kensing grabs hold of Terrin again. Grabbing him by the arm, he throws him across the room again. Landing on a table, he hits his back just right.

Hitting the corner of the table he feels the pain in his back as it throbs and aches. Looking up he sees Kensing coming for him again. Looking on the table for anything, he throws a glass beaker at Kensing. Sailing across the room the beaker breaks, as it smashes against Kensing's face and cuts it. Smiling as he comes, Kensing reaches out and takes hold of Terrin's arm again.

Throwing him against the far wall, Terrin falls to the floor as he moans. Grabbing a corner of a table, he falls down. As he hits the floor again, the remote slips out of his pocket. As it falls out, it activates, showing a doorway behind Kensing. Taking a deep breath, he gets ready. As Kensing comes closer, he smiles at Terrin.

Holding the remote in one hand, he braces himself with the other. Waiting for Kensing to get within reach, he lies there breathing hard as he comes closer. Getting into range, Terrin speaks up and says, "I love you man", as his foot comes up and connects with Kensing's chest, squarely.

Hitting the button that activates the doorway Kensing goes backward and falls into the doorway. Closing the doorway before he can come back through, he goes over and sees about Missy. During the battle, she got hit by a stray shard of glass. Turning her over, Terrin sees it sticking out of her neck.

"NOOOOOOOO", Terrin shouts.

CHAPTER 22

Hearing the commotion downstairs, everyone comes running to see what is happening. Going down the stairs, they get to the bottom. Looking around, they see the lab trashed. Everything is broke or spilled, or just turned over. Looking into a far corner they see Terrin, cradling Missy's lifeless form, as he cries.

"What happened?" Tabrinia and Tanya ask as one.

"Kensing went crazy. He tried to kill me. I guess he killed Missy instead. I don't know what got into him", Terrin explains.

"Where is he?" Tabrinia asks.

"Who... Kensing? I opened a doorway behind him and kicked him in. I don't know where he went though" Terrin replies sheepishly, as he wipes the tears from his eyes.

"Well... Now what are we going to do?" Tabrinia asks.

"I don't know", Terrin says. "Anyone have any suggestions?" Terrin asks.

"Well... We could hide her and not say

anything", Tanya offers up.

"Where do you get this kind of crap from?" he asks her.

"From t.v.", she replies smartly.

"That figures. HRS tells you, you have to let your kids watch t.v. and look what they learn. No wonder we have so many criminals in society. It's people letting kids read books that are not good, like this one", Terrin replies.

"What do you suggest?" Tabrinia asks.

"I don't know. I suppose we could.... Ahhhh.... You know.... What she said", he replies pointing at Tanya.

"You are worse than I am, dad", Tanya says.

"It was your suggestion. Not mine", he says.

"That doesn't matter. You are willing to go through with it", Tanya replies.

"Okay... Let's just do it and get it over with", Terrin replies.

Carrying her body up the stairs, Terrin carries her outside. Taking her around the house, he finds a place where it would be far enough away. Telling Tabrinia to go get him a shovel, he puts Missy's body down. Waiting for Tabrinia to come back, she finally comes back, with a couple of shovels. Handing one to Terrin, he starts digging. Digging a hole big enough for her body to fit in, he digs down, until he figures it is deep enough.

Rolling her body over, he rolls her into the hole. Shoveling the dirt back in over her, he finishes, as he spreads the rest of the dirt all over, to make it look like it was. Standing there after he is done, he says, "Let's bow our heads and say a few words", he says. "Dear heavenly father...we are gathered here today, to ask you to forgive this girl... She didn't know what she was getting into. Don't hold her responsible for my actions".

"GOD... If you can hear us, please be kind and fair with Missy", Tanya says.

"And take good care of her. She was a very bright and intelligent girl. May her memory live in our souls forever.... Amen", Terrin says as his eyes start watering again.

Looking up at the rest of them, he sees they are crying to. Coming together, they all hug as one. Looking back down at Missy's grave, they head back into the house. Sitting on the couch, Terrin just sits and stares at nothing. "Terrin, babe... You can't blame yourself", Tabrinia says.

Staring straight ahead, Terrin doesn't respond in any way, shape or form. Sitting down next to him, Tabrinia talks and whispers to him until she falls asleep. Tanya comes in and sits down across from them. Looking at him she starts thinking she is going to lose her Father, as well. Shaking her head, she hopes and prays it is not true.

She watches him until he falls asleep. Going into her room, she gets the patches out and peels one off the foil. Placing it on her Fathers arm, she peels off three more and places them on his arm. Waking up, Terrin starts going into convulsions. Grabbing his stomach and bending over, he falls on the floor. Looking up he mouths the words, how could you?

Watching in horror, Terrin watches as Tanya

transforms into one of those creatures, from hell. Laughing as it changes, it grabs Tabrinia and takes her away. A few minutes later, the pain stops and Terrin has this glazed over look to his eyes. Feeling more powerful than he has ever felt he gets up and tries to locate the thing. Looking all around, he senses something, in a southerly direction.

Running in that direction he feels the creature close by. As the drug takes a stronger hold, his face starts bubbling out. Growing odd and misshapen, he is soon a creature himself. As his fear and anger overwhelm him, he almost forgets about Tabrinia. Continuing on, he sees the creature with Tabrinia. Catching up he stands in front of the creature and says in a booming voice, "Put her down. How dare you take my girl... Do you know who I am? You fool. I am the god killer", he roars as he smacks the creature and flings him across the clearing.

Standing back up, the creature runs at him. Getting near, Terrin grabs him by the arms and throws him against a tree. Hearing bones crack and muscle tear apart, the creature gets back up and runs again. Throwing him against a tree and repeatedly smashing his face into it he finally quits, when he thinks the creature is almost dead.

Standing back up, Terrin looks at the creature and thinking about its head exploding… It happens. The creature's head explodes, covering everything with demon brains. Gathering Tabrinia up, he takes her back to the house. Feeling a strength he has never felt before, his anger starts to rise. Getting angry, he starts roaring out in animal pain. Feeling betrayed he roars again.

Going into Tanya's room, he finds the rest of the patches. Getting an evil grin on his face, he smiles the most gruesome smile, as he puts the patches all over his body. A few minutes later, his body is being wracked with painful, stomachaches. His body feels like it is on fire. Screaming out in primal rage, the pain suddenly ceases. Standing up, he walks out of the house and away from it. Walking mindlessly as his anger builds up, he gets more and more pissed off.

As the drugs take their full effect on him, he gets to a point where he cannot bear to live anymore. Putting his hand into his pocket he pulls out the remote and looks at it. As the reality dawns on him of what he is holding, he starts smiling evilly again. Laughing in a deep, baritone voice, he looks for a doorway.

Not seeing any in the immediate vicinity, he starts wandering around. Not being able to find one, he starts getting really pissed off. Running through the trees in a blind rage, he accidentally opens a doorway and goes through. Continuing to run, he finally looks up and sees clouds all over the place. As the rage builds in him, he feels invincible.

Running through the clouds, his rage builds as he runs. Not caring what gets in his way, he just runs and runs. He runs for what seems like days, before realizing that he is getting nowhere. Waking up, Tabrinia has a splitting headache.

Looking around, she wonders where everyone is. Looking through the house, she remembers what happened to Missy and Kensing. Then, Tanya turned into a creature. "Is this some kind of nightmare", she thinks.

Going out into the kitchen, she can't find anyone. Going outside, she goes over and opens the lab up. Going downstairs she starts turning the systems on. Getting it all set up and ready to go, she manually sets up the coordinates that were written on a piece of paper. Powering the doorway up, she hits the fail-safe and activates the doorway.

Jumping through, she looks around and sees she is in the clouds. "TERRIN", she yells out.

Looking around she can't see anyone, or anything. Walking along, she continues to look for anyone. Just a glimpse of something would even be nice. Walking for hours, she never even comes close to seeing anything, or anyone.

As he was running, he looked up and saw some things coming at him, from above. As they get closer, he sees they are angels.

"GET BACK...... I HAVE COME TO TAKE OVER", Terrin roars out in a titanic voice, that booms out and rolls like thunder.

Shrinking away slightly, they start coming forward. One comes forward as the others stay back. "Excuse me sir... But I don't think you know what you are doing", he replies.

"OH BUT I DO", his voice booms out.

"What do you want?" he asks.

"I WANT TO TAKE OVER", he roars out.

Walking forward, Terrin grabs the angel and throws him against the ground. Hearing the bone breaking as he smashes the angel into the ground, he watches as the wing is ripped away. Looking at the other angels, Terrin gets some serious thoughts brewing in his head. Smiling wickedly, he throws balls of flame at the angels, burning them to cinders instantly.

Walking forward, with more determination than ever before, he aims to find this being that is in charge and take him out. Stomping as his face gets even more contorted, he keeps walking, no matter how serious the pain. Not letting it affect him, he just knows he is going to kill someone, before his life is over.

Seeing a commotion up ahead, she starts running towards it. Looking at it, she sees flames coming from it. Wondering what is happening, she knows it must be Terrin whatever he was doing. Running on she hears a sound from behind her. Looking over her shoulder, she sees an angel trying to swoop down and whisk her away. Ducking as it gets close, she avoids the angel for awhile.

Running to where she thinks Terrin is, the angel comes in and tries again. Turning around, she brings her foot up and kicks the angel squarely in the face. Falling down unconscious, the angel lands in a pile and doesn't move. Turning around, she starts running again towards the fire. Hearing a thunderous boom, she covers her ears, as it is so loud.

CHAPTER 23

Continuing towards the fire, she hears another noise, behind her. Looking back, she is ready to deal with the stupid angel again. What she sees, stops her dead in her tracks. Looking at her, with the most awful face and meanest stare ever, she stares at GOD. When he speaks, his voice is soft, yet firm and stern.

"How dare you invade my domain. I made you. You do as I say. How did you get here?" he asks.

"How dare you talk to me like that. I didn't ask to be born. That was your idea. And as for how I got here, I'm not going to tell you, cause if you were GOD, you would already know", she replies in as firm and in control voice.

"How dare you speak to me like that", he says. "Now you will pay for invading my domain", as he starts to point his finger at her.

From out of nowhere, they hear a thunderous boom, as the clouds split into two. After the clouds split, they hear, "DON"T YOU DARE TOUCH HER.OR ELSE", Terrin states sternly.

"And who do you think you are?" GOD asks.

"I AM YOUR WORST NIGHTMARE. A MORTAL...... COMING TO KILL HIS CREATOR", as he shows up between the split clouds.

Looking on him with a strange look, GOD asks, "What makes you think you can take me on?"

"BECAUSE..... I CAN DO WHAT YOU CAN ONLY DREAM ABOUT", Terrin replies as he laughs creating a loud boom.

"You are nothing but a mere mortal. You are nothing to me", GOD says as if addressing a puny audience.

"HOW DARE YOU TALK TO ME THAT WAY", Terrin replies as he flings a bolt of electrical energy at GOD and hits his face.

Searing his face, the bolt leaves a mark on him. Reaching up with his hand, he feels the furrow the bolt caused. Pulling his hand away, he sees some kind of fluid on them. His blood… As he thinks. "How dare you treat me like that. NOW YOU WILL PAY THE PRICE", God's voice booms out as he flings a bolt of lightning at Terrin.

Missing him he turns and follows it, to make sure it doesn't attack from behind. Raising his hand, he fires a flaming ball of fire at GOD and hits him in the arm. Searing the flesh, GOD shrieks out in pain. "OH... SO YOU CAN BE HURT", Terrin says as he laughs. "SOME GOD YOU ARE", he adds.

"NOW YOU WILL PAY THE PRICE", GOD states as he fires a ball of electricity at Terrin, hitting him in the arm.

Searing his flesh as it hits him, he grabs his arm with his other hand and thinks for a second. Taking his hand away, the mark is gone. Smiling more wickedly than ever before, he flings another fireball at GOD. Hitting him directly in the face, it burns his face away, leaving nothing but a burn ward victim's face.

Screaming out in pain and rage, GOD runs towards him and grabs him by the throat. Throwing him across half of heaven, Terrin hits something hard and smashes against it. Getting up, he starts back toward GOD. Getting to him, they engage in another battle. Flying towards GOD, Terrin hits him in the chest. Knocking him across heaven, you can hear thunder rumble, as GOD rolls across the clouds.

Coming to a stop, he gets up and heads back towards Terrin. Getting to him, he rushes him and knocks Terrin to the ground. Flinging bolt after bolt of electricity, Terrin is soon nothing but a mass of formerly human flesh. Turning his back on Terrin, GOD turns around and confronts Tabrinia. Demanding to know what she is doing here and how she got here, she doesn't say anything.

Having some angels take her away, he is knocked to the ground. Looking back up he sees Terrin, with eyes so red, they burn deep into God's own soul. Experiencing fear for the first time in his life, he shakes slightly as Terrin flings ball after ball of fire. Turning GOD into a pulpy mass of flesh, he takes Tabrinia's hand and starts to lead her away from this massive destruction.

Getting to within a mile of the doorway, GOD comes from behind and tackles Terrin to the ground. Getting up as GOD flings balls of lightning and electricity at him, he defends himself with self-preservation. Bringing his body back to normal, Terrin gets up and grabs GOD by the throat. Squeezing until he sees his head starts to turn purple, he pops his head off, like a ripe melon.

Slamming his body against the ground, he smashes it and smashes it, until he is pretty sure he is dead. Taking Tabrinia by the hand, he leads her to the doorway. Taking the remote out of his pocket, he activates the doorway locator. Seeing the doorway, he is just about to open it, when GOD comes up behind him and starts pummeling him, with bigger balls of power and flame.

Dropping the remote, Tabrinia picks it up and checks it out. Watching as Terrin and GOD fight, she is amazed that he can even be hurt, or put down. Having a whole new view on GOD, she decides that he is as mortal as anyone else is. Just a little more powerful. Kicking him in the chest as he lays on the ground, GOD rises up and then comes slamming against the ground.

Getting back up, GOD turns around and looks at Terrin. "I DON'T KNOW WHERE YOU GOT YOUR POWER FROM.... BUT I AM THE MOST POWERFUL FORCE EVER CREATED.. I AM GOING TO SNUFF YOU OUT LIKE A LIGHT BULB", GOD says as he smashes his hand into Terrin's face and through it.

As his face gets smashed, Terrin falls to the ground. Thinking Terrin is dead and not capable of recovering from the last hit, GOD looks down at Tabrinia and starts dealing with her. Turning his back to Terrin, he doesn't see as he gets back up. Telling Tabrinia to locate a doorway, he says he is going to kick GOD and she has to open, then close the doorway, quickly. Nodding her head in understanding, she gets ready.

Turning the locator on, Terrin smiles as he sees it behind GOD. Mentally changing the settings with his mind, Tabrinia says, "Hey.... Look behind you".

Turning around, Tabrinia opens the doorway as Terrin kicks him squarely in the chest. Flying through the air, GOD flies through the doorway, as Tabrinia closes it. Laughing as loud as the thunder itself, the clouds start losing their mass. They start melting, as if they never existed. Turning around, he sees all the angels gathered around him, looking at him.

Speaking, Terrin says, "HEY YOU SCREWUPS.... THERE IS A NEW RULER IN TOWN... AND HIS NAME IS", as he gets hit from behind.

Falling face first into a cloud, Terrin turns around and sees a mass of angel's break apart. Smiling at them, he flings balls of electricity and fire at the angels. Flaming their wings on fire, they fall to the ground as they are burned off. Taking care of the angels that hit him, he continues, "AND HIS NAME IS TERRIN... ANYONE ELSE THAT DECIDES THEY WANT TO CHALLENGE ME, WILL BE SENT

STRAIGHT TO HELL".

Smiling at him Tabrinia says, "Are you sure this is all right? I mean... What if you actually kill him, then what?"

"What harm can it do. We are just letting him know that if he can't do the job right, then we will", as he starts laughing the wickedest laugh he has ever laughed.

Flying through the air, he looks around and finds himself in a very red and not so very nice place. As soon as he hit the ground and made a ruckus, demons from all over swarm him and start tearing him, limb from limb. Screaming out in rage and pain, GOD sees SATAN coming for him. Smiling as he approaches, SATAN raises an arm and dismisses all his minions.

"WHAT DID I TELL YOU BROTHER?" SATAN asks.

"YOU SAID, IF I EVER SHOW MY FACE IN YOUR DOMAIN... YOU WOULD MAKE ME SORRY", GOD replies.

"THAT'S RIGHT. AND DO YOU KNOW WHAT TIME IT IS?" he asks with a smile on his face.

"IT'S THAT TIME?" GOD asks.

Nodding his head up and down, SATAN grabs him and nails him to a cross in the middle of his kingdom. Letting all his minions and slaves view him, they all cheer the devil on. Seeing GOD put up on display, Kensing shakes his head and knows something is terribly wrong. Going over to GOD, Kensing waits in ambush, until the coast is clear.

When everyone and everything leaves,

Kensing approaches and starts taking the bindings loose. Getting down from the upside down cross, GOD follows Kensing. Getting far enough away from the center, Kensing opens the doorway with his mind. Walking through the doorway, they find themselves in heaven again.

Seeing Terrin up ahead, Kensing and GOD talk and make a plan. Approaching Terrin from the front, GOD starts sending bolts of lightning at him. Hitting him repeatedly, he knocks Terrin to the ground. Coming up from behind him, Kensing pummels him from behind. Turning him into a mass of nothing, Kensing and GOD shake hands.

Taking Tabrinia by the hand, he leads her to the doorway and takes her back through. Looking down, GOD sees the mass start moving. Watching as it reassembles itself back into human shape, GOD can't believe this mortal. Creating a cage, he places it around Terrin. As his body is totally created, he gets up and tries to use his powers.

Finding his powers all gone, he screams out in rage. "You can't do this to me".

"But I already have. I am GOD. To me, you are nothing. I can't kill you, but I can stop you from doing harm to anyone else. You will be on display for eternity", GOD says as he starts laughing.

Getting angrier, Terrin balls his hand into a fist and slams it into his other hand. "I will get loose... And when I do... You will pay the price", Terrin states.

"HAHAHAAHAHAHA...... You'll never get

close", GOD says.

"We'll see", Terrin replies.

"What... Do you think you are a god?" as he laughs at Terrin.

"No.... I'm one of your creations... But you don't seem to understand... Everyone, no matter what, can die. Even a creator of worlds", Terrin replies smiling wickedly.

"This won't happen again. I can promise you that", GOD says, as he turns away and walks to his throne.

Touching parts of the sky, he starts making motions in the air, with his hands. Seeing something form at his fingertips, the earth appears in front of him. Touching different spots on the world, Terrin sees small spots light up. "What are you doing?" he demands to know.

"You will never know", GOD replies.

"I think I already know", Terrin says smiling slightly.

"Mayhap you do", GOD replies.

Watching on, he sees things happening on the planet's surface. Screaming out in rage, Terrin's voice roars out like it did before. "NOOOOOOOOOOOOOOOOOOOOOOOOOOOOO".

Turning to him, GOD has a look of fear in his eyes. Watching in horror as Terrin bends the bars and steps out, his mouth falls open. "NOW... YOU HAVE PISSED ME OFF", Terrin says as he flings a ball of flame so big, it almost encompasses half of heaven.

Burning God's body, he watches as it is turned into a pile of ashes. Creating a wind, the ashes blow away in different directions. Turning towards the throne, Terrin sits in the chair and smiles. As a hand reaches around the chair, it grabs him by the throat and starts strangling the life from him.

Reaching up with his hands, he tries to pull away the hands. Not being very successful, he is suddenly wrenched away and out of the chair. Ripping his head from his body, he tears the body into small pieces. Looking up, you can see the blood lust in God's eyes. Smiling evilly, he finishes with the body and has the angels dispose of the remains. Getting his composure back, he goes back to the planet that hangs there in the air.

When they arrive back at the lab, they find the lab a mess. Looking around, they see all the components trashed. Hearing a noise from upstairs, they go up and see Tanya, smashing anything in her way. "Tanya", Tabrinia says.

Turning around, she says, "What?"

"What are you doing. Have you gone crazy?"

"No... My dad went crazy. I hate this world", she says as she continues to smash whatever happens to be in reach.

"Tanya... It's not your fault", Tabrinia says. "Calm down... Let's talk about this".

Looking at her, she drops the club. "I'm sorry", she says as she starts to cry.

"That's all right. We all need to get it out sometimes", as she holds her in her arms.

Reaching up to scratch an itch, Kensing starts ripping the patches off. Taking them all off, he starts feeling better. Smiling as he feels great, he walks over and joins the girls. Hearing a trumpeting sound in the air, he looks up and sees a bunch of angels, coming down, carrying something in their hands.

Putting his arms around the girls, he leads them away from the house. Helping them into the truck, they drive away from the worst place, they have ever encountered. Driving away, none of them look back. Heading into town Tabrinia asks, "What are we going to say about Terrin and Missy being gone?" Tabrinia asks.

"I don't know. We can always tell them we don't know where they are. Hey... Maybe they left and we haven't seen them since?" Kensing suggests.

Laughing, Tanya says, "Yeah... Like anyone is going to believe that story", as she laughs.

"You never know. We can't very well tell them that GOD killed Terrin and Missy got killed by accident, in a fight between me and Terrin", Kensing says.

PART 2

THE POWER WITHIN

HELL ON EARTH

"Hey... Tanya, how did you get back anyway?" Kensing asks, curiously.

"I thought I told you... I just all of a sudden... Looked around... And I was in the lab", she explains.

"Yeah... But how do we know it's really you, this time?" Tabrinia asks.

"Just trust me... Please. I just know it's me", she replies.

"Okay... We'll give you the benefit of the doubt...... This time", Kensing says.

"Ohhh... Wait. I forgot my necklace... The one my dad gave me for my fifth birthday. Can we please go back and get it?" Tanya asks with a look of desperation in her eyes.

"Sure, why not?" Kensing says as he turns the truck around and heads for the house again.

Arriving back at the house, they see the lab doors wide open. The house looks evil, as it sits there and almost seems to grin. Jumping out of the truck as they approach the house, she runs down into the lab. Waiting for her to return, they talk and discuss what they should do. They decide upon leaving the country and going to Mexico.

Sensing something not right Kensing says, "Something's wrong.... I have the feeling Tanya is in trouble", as he shakes his head.

Cutting the engine off, they get out and head down to the lab. "Tanya?" Kensing asks out.

Not getting a reply, they see the pyramid... It looks like the doorway is open. But the glow is faint, as if it weren't open all the way, but just a sliver. Looking around, Kensing feels something behind him. Turning around, he comes face to face with one of those creatures from hell. Using his mind, he makes them stay back. "Tabrinia.... We have... Ummm... Company", Kensing says as she turns around.

Turning around, she sees five of the creatures. Staring at them, she watches as they try to come forward. But they have no luck. "How did you get here?" Kensing asks the creatures.

Not getting a reply, he asks Tabrinia, "I can almost bet these bastards have taken Tanya back through the doorway", he states.

"What gives you that idea?" Tabrinia asks.

"Because she is not here and they are", he replies, as he goes over and looks at the pyramid. "Tabrinia, is there anything you can do with what's left?" he asks.

"I'm not sure. I will have to see what there is to work with", she replies as she starts looking at the pyramid and seeing the damage isn't as bad as she thought.

"If you need any help... Just let me know. I am

going to hold these bastards off", Kensing says as he keeps the creatures at bay.

Working on the doorway, Tabrinia finds almost everything she needs to get it back in working order. Replacing the parts she has, she makes a small list up, as to what she will need to fix it. Giving the list to Kensing, he looks at her with a funny look in his eyes. "Don't look at me", he says as he shrugs his shoulders.

Shaking her head, she starts looking around, trying to see if there just happens to be anything around. Finding one part, she installs it and then starts looking for the other two parts. "I'm going into the house. I want to see if he has anything stashed inside", she says as she heads upstairs.

"Okay... I will keep these... These... Things back", Kensing replies as he keeps his mind control up.

Running up the stairs, Tabrinia goes into the house and looks around for any, or all of the parts. Not finding anything up in the attic, she goes into the basement and looks around. Bumping into a wall, it opens and reveals a stash of components. Finding a box, she places as much into the box as she can and heads back to the lab.

Getting into the lab, she takes out the two components she needed. Installing them into the pyramid, she puts it back together again. Finishing it up, she turns the power on and hears the system come online. "Computer.... Give me a readout on the doorway", Tabrinia says.

"No way. I don't have to", the computer replies, as it starts making laughing noises.

"Readout in progress", it adds, a moment later.

Waiting for the computer to get done, they talk and ask each other what they should do. Saying they are going to have to go to hell again, they decide they will try to set the doorway to open in twenty-four hours. Agreeing, the computer says, "Readout available on screen".

Going over to the monitor, Tabrinia looks at the figures and starts inputting the figures that appear at the head of the list. Starting the initiation sequence, she activates the doorway. As the green light fills the room, it starts turning a dark, deep, red color. "Ummm... Tabrinia. What's happening?" Kensing asks.

Shaking her head she says, "I don't know".

Using his brain, Kensing forces the creatures' back into the doorway. After the creatures are through the doorway, Kensing goes over and sticks his head in. Looking around, he sees it's the right place. "Okay... This is it. Set the computer up to open the doorway in twenty-four hours".

"Okay... If you think we should do this?" Tabrinia replies as she grimaces slightly.

"We have to. I can't leave her there. I couldn't live with myself", Kensing says.

"Okay.... Computer... Open doorway for twenty-five seconds then activate the self-startup system. Set it for twenty-four hours. If no one comes through within.... Let's say an hour. Then every twenty-four hours thereafter until we come back", Tabrinia says to the computer.

"Initiating startup..... Opening doorway.... Setting auto-turn on.... Fifteen seconds to open doorway...... Ten seconds..... Please be ready", the computer says.

Getting prepared to jump into the doorway, Kensing looks at Tabrinia and they both have odd looks on their faces. "Doorway... Open", the computer says.

Jumping through, they find themselves in hell. Again. Walking along and trying to find Tanya, they hope they can get her back, for real this time. Making small talk and discussing the current situation they see a small bunch of creatures and decide to walk the opposite way. As they walk on, they see the wheel again.

"I know where the maze is at", Kensing says as he leads her towards the maze.

"Is that where she's at?" Tabrinia asks.

"I guess. It seems to be the place they like to store people. Me and Terrin were in here before", Kensing says.

"Okay.... Let's go... I guess", she says.

Turning to the left of the wheel, Kensing leads her to the maze. Walking the same way that him and Terrin went, they find themselves in the maze. "Okay... Here's the deal.... We need to keep track of which way we turn", he replies.

"I can do that. I have a pretty good memory", Tabrinia replies, as she smiles.

Walking along, they follow a different route than he has been before. Looking into rooms, they see some more strange stuff going on. Gagging a few times, Tabrinia says, "Why didn't you tell me.... About... These rooms?"

"I'm sorry... I forgot", he says.

"That's all right... I can deal with it now",

Tabrinia replies.

Walking and turning corners, they turn one corner too many. As they come around a corner, they see the massive dude that chased Kensing and Terrin before. "Ohhh shit", Kensing says as he tries to turn around.

Bumping into Tabrinia, he tries to drag her back around the corner. "What... What is it?" she asks.

"It's a big, bad ass dude", Kensing says.

"Can you stop him?" she asks.

"I'm not sure if I still can.... I don't have any patches on... And my powers don't seem as strong as they do as when I have a patch on", he says.

"Ohhh... Okay", she replies as she smiles.

"You should know", he adds a moment later.

"I know... I'm just messing with you", she replies as she tries to make light of the situation.

"That's all right... Paybacks a bitch", Kensing says as he smiles.

Smiling back, she nods her head. Walking back the way they came, they go a different way. Searching for what seems like hours, Kensing looks at his watch. Raising his eyebrows, he says, "We have about sixteen hours before the doorway opens".

"We need to find her and fast", Tabrinia says.

Turning various corners, they wander around and look into rooms. Not finding her, they start to head back. Turning a corner, they come face to face, with the big badass dude, himself. Shaking his head, Kensing hopes he can hold this dude off. Trying with all his might, he tries to erect a barrier. Coming forward, the creature comes to a stop as it hits the barrier.

Laughing as he watches, Kensing says, "C'mon... We need to get out of here".

Running back the way they came, they see Tanya up ahead. She is being led by four of the creatures. Following after them, Kensing looks over his shoulder and doesn't see the big dude. As they get closer to the creatures with Tanya, the creatures see them and two of them turn around. Eyeing them as they approach, the creatures can't believe they are coming forward.

Thinking about an invisible bulldozer pushing them back, they start moving backwards. Looking around for anything that might be pushing them, they look at each other and start to tear each other limb from limb. Watching as the creatures dismember each other, they soon fall down but continue trying to kill the other one.

Moving around them, Kensing and Tabrinia look down corridors as they go. Spotting her down a hallway, Kensing says, "Down there", as he points.

Running as fast as they can they soon catch up with them. Staying back about twenty-five feet, they watch and see where they are taking her. Following them for what seems a couple of hours, they watch as they take her into a room. Entering the room, they see the big, badass dude himself. "Well.... Well.... Well... What do we have here?" the dude asks.

"Ummmm... Nothing. Not a thing", Kensing replies as he starts to smile.

"What are you doing in my domain?" he asks.

"We just happened to be in the neighborhood and thought, we might stop by.... You know and just say, HI", Kensing replies in a smart-ass tone.

"Don't patronize me. You have already doomed yourselves to spend eternity here. You have no choice anymore.... Unless......", the dude says.

"Unless what?" Kensing dares to ask.

"Unless you open the doorway permanently", he says.

"Wait a minute.... Why can't you open the doorway?" Kensing asks as he starts smiling.

"You have to do it. It has to be opened by a mortal", he replies.

"And if we say.... NO... Then what?" Kensing asks.

"Then you can just stay here forever", the demon says.

"And if we open the doorway.... Then we will still be here, cause you will take all this over", Kensing says. "I don't see any reason to open it for you. There's nothing in it for us, except to stay in hell".

"Yeah... But you will be left alone and can do as you wish", the demon replies.

Shaking his head Kensing says, "I don't know.... That's a decision I can't make by myself", as he turns to Tabrinia and gives her his, don't agree with me look.

"No way. Don't even look at me. This is solely your decision", Tabrinia says.

"Bring me Tanya and let me see what she says", Kensing says to the demon.

"Very well. Guards, bring the girl", he says as he smiles down on Kensing.

Leading her in are four creatures. Bringing her to Kensing, he asks, "Have you heard what we have been talking about?"

"No. I haven't", she replies as she shakes her head.

Relating to her what the demon has proposed, she asks, "You didn't agree..... Did you?" as her eyes open wide up.

"I haven't agreed to anything... Yet", he says.

"Don't... He just wants to take over and bring hell to Earth", she replies. "I can feel it".

Looking at the creatures holding Tanya, Kensing pushes them away as he grabs Tanya's hand and drags her towards Tabrinia. Trying to hold the demons back, Kensing tells them to go. I will be with you in a minute he says. Running down the corridor, Tabrinia and Tanya run like the wind. Backing up as he keeps the creatures at bay, he gets to the door and turns and runs as he looks away.

Running and looking over his shoulder, he watches the way the girls go and follows them. Seeing them up ahead, he continues on until he finally catches up with them. Rushing them down the corridor, they take the turns they think is the way and run. Running for an endless time, they are soon out of breath and stop to catch their breath.

While they are walking in circles, Kensing looks the way they just came and sees a bunch of creatures coming down it. "Ummmm... Girls. I think it's time we split", Kensing says as he points down the corridor.

Following his finger, they see the creatures and start running again. Looking behind them every now and then, Kensing looks back and trips. Falling down, he sees the bunch coming faster and faster. Getting up he runs like he's never run before. Catching up with the girls, he passes them and turns right. Grabbing the girls as they go by, he pulls them in.

Putting his finger to his lips, he whispers, "Shhhhhh".

Nodding their heads, they stay quiet. Watching, he points to a door. Going to the door, they go in while Kensing stays there. Waiting for the creatures, he makes the room look empty. As the creatures near the door, they start slowing down. Looking into rooms, they go past and continue looking for them.

Going to the door, he opens it and whispers, "I think it's safe now. C'mon".

Going with Kensing, they go out into the hallway and go in the opposite direction as the creatures. Walking down the corridor, they make the next turn and start making the turns they were supposed to. Going with instinct and intuition, Kensing just keeps going and turning corners at random it seems.

Turning once more, they see a dead-end up ahead. "Kensing... Now what?" Tabrinia and Tanya ask together.

"Don't worry. It's a fake wall", he says. "Me and Terrin found out the last time we were here".

"Okay... If you say so", Tabrinia says.

Running to the wall, Kensing smacks face first

into it. Slamming into the wall at such speed just made it that much worse. As he slammed into the wall, his face got totally ragged out. He slammed into it, and then fell backward, onto the ground. Groaning as he lies there while his face is all bloody, the girls tear up their shirtsleeves and start trying to clean his face off.

Getting the worst of it, Kensing shakes his head and says, "Ouch.... Damn that hurts".

"Stay down for a minute. Let me finish cleaning your face off. Okay?" Tabrinia asks.

"Okay, okay", he replies.

Wiping his face off, they finally get most of the bleeding to stop. Seeing that it has a lot of little dots in it, Tanya starts laughing as Tabrinia asks, "What?"

"His face.... Look at his face. It looks like a ‘connect the dot’ picture", she replies as she continues to laugh.

"Hey... C’mon, haven't I been hurt enough already?" Kensing asks.

"I'm sorry... It's just that it hit me just right", Tanya replies.

"I know what you mean", he says.

Getting up, Kensing feels the wall. Touching it, his hand goes through it. "What the..." he starts saying.

Laughing as she sees his hand go through it, Tabrinia joins her. Kensing looks at them both as he starts laughing too. Walking through the wall, they follow him. Getting to the other side of the wall, they find themselves back by the original location. Smiling as they see where they are, Kensing looks at his watch. "We've only got ten minutes. Let's go", he says.

Going back to where they think the doorway is, they wait. In the meantime, they don't seem to notice a band of creatures coming up from behind them. Looking at his watch, Kensing shakes his head and then says, "Man... Something doesn't feel right".

"Hmmm.... Oh, yeah. I feel it to", Tabrinia agrees.

"I feel it too", Tanya says as well.

Turning around, Tanya screams as she sees all the creatures coming from behind. Looking around, Kensing tries to use his power but it doesn't seem to have an effect on them. They keep coming. "Tabrinia, help me. Use your power and combine with mine and see if we can hold them off", Kensing says.

"Okay", as she starts concentrating with him.

When the creatures get to within ten feet of them, they are stopped. Trying to push their way through, they get a few more feet, but can't seem to get any farther. Roaring with all they've got, they try their damnedest to get past it. Looking behind the creatures, Kensing nods and whispers, "Behind them", as she looks and sees the doorway starting to open.

Walking forward, they start pushing the creatures back. Pushing them past the doorway Kensing says, "As soon as we get back, someone has to turn the power off".

Nodding her head in agreement, they jump through. As they get into the lab, Tabrinia says, "Computer... Shut doorway... Now".

"Doorway closing... Doorway closed", but not

before three creatures make it through.

Trying to use his powers, Kensing just doesn't have enough left in him. Looking around quickly, he sees a metal pipe lying on the floor. Bending down, he picks it up and smashes it upside one of the creature's heads. When the pipe hit the creatures head, it sunk in about three inches and some kind of black, pus-like stuff started squirting out. Getting a whiff of the stench, Kensing almost falls down.

Covering his nose, he starts swinging at the other ones. When Tabrinia saw the creatures come through, she panicked and ran. She ran up the stairs and ran away. Tanya saw a knife lying on the table and lanced one of the creature's arms. As the black, pus-like stuff squirted out of him, a little got on Tanya's arm and started burning through.

Screaming in pain as she slashes at the creature blindly, she lances its throat wide open. Roaring out, the sound fades away rather quickly as his head falls back and exposes his insides. Seeing things wriggling around in their, Tanya turns away and runs. She runs up the stairs and outside.

Clubbing the last one, it gets a lucky hit in and knocks Kensing to his knees. Striking out at the creature as he falls down, he swings the club and manages to hit the creature in the knees. While the creature roars out in pain, Kensing swings again and hits the creature in the head. As the black, pus-like stuff comes out, Kensing stands up and runs up the stairs.

Looking for Tabrinia and Tanya, he doesn't

see them anywhere outside and assumes they are in the house. Going into the house, he finds them. They are in the basement, cowering in a corner. "Hey... Girls... You can come out now. All the creatures are dead", he says as he tries to coax them out.

Seeing them stand up from behind one of the tables, he starts laughing. "What's so damn funny?" Tabrinia asks as she gives him a mean look.

"You guys are. I can't believe you wouldn't help me Tabrinia. At least Tanya took one of the creatures out before she left", Kensing replies as he continues to laugh.

"I can't help it. I was scared after all that we have been through", Tabrinia says as she starts to get angry.

"You don't need to get mad. We are only playing with you", Kensing replies as he goes over and tries to hug her.

Pushing him away she says, "Leave me alone. I don't want nothing to do with you", as she runs up the stairs and out the front door.

"Tabrinia", Kensing starts to say. "What's her problem?" Kensing asks Tanya.

"I don't know", as she shakes her head. "I'll find out though", as she runs up the stairs and out the door after Tabrinia.

Looking around, Kensing starts making more of the stuff that he made before. Mixing up the things he needs to make his special patches, he gets fifteen of them made by the time Tanya has Tabrinia calmed down and convinced they were not really laughing at her. Coming down the stairs Tabrinia says, "I'm sorry. I didn't mean to run out like that. Sometimes I just can't help it. Can you forgive me?" she asks as she looks down at the floor

"Of course I forgive you. You didn't do anything to be forgiven for..... Really", Kensing replies as they hug each other.

"Thanks", she says. "What are you doing anyway?" she asks.

"I was preparing in case some of them creatures are still here. I don't trust anything else anymore", Kensing says as he shows them all the patches he has made up.

"Let me have one", Tabrinia says.

"I can't do that. They are made for me and me only. I made a designer patch for whoever's DNA was used. Sorry", Kensing says.

"That's all right. Can you make some for me, so I can help in case there are still some of them around?" Tabrinia asks as she gives him her sad eyes.

"Hang on. Let me get some DNA from your arm. Once I have that, I can make a set for you", he replies as he smiles at her.

Smiling back she says, "If I can help in any way, let me know".

"Okay. Give me twenty-five minutes and then I can have you help me", he says as he starts to get the DNA from her arm.

Preparing everything he needs to get the mixture started, he tells Tabrinia what she needs to do and how to do it. Nodding her head as she follows his directions, she gets done with the mixture. Taking it over to Kensing, he looks at it and nods as he takes it and adds something to it and then prepares it for the patch process.

Putting it in his machine, he waits as it gets done. Taking it out, he makes the patches as he finishes the last part of the process. Making the patches, he gets done and puts them in the freezer for a few seconds. Timing the last procedure, he takes them out and hands them to Tabrinia and tells her to be used only if necessary. Agreeing with him, she takes them and puts them in her pocket.

Turning around, her arm hits a bottle of acid. As it falls to the floor, she backs up and hits a rack of shelves. Knocking them over, she runs up the stairs and out the front door. Shaking his head, Kensing follows her and finally catches her. Grabbing her arm he asks, "What the hell was that?"

"I'm sorry. My arm bumped the acid and I was backing away, so I wouldn't get splashed, when I hit the shelves and I just had to get out of there, before something else went wrong", she explains.

"That's all right. Accidents happen. Look at me. I have had accidents. It's a part of life. If you didn't make a mistake, you'd be a robot", Kensing says to her as he hugs her.

Looking at him, she smiles and hugs him back. Heading back to the house, they turn around and see Tanya running towards them. "Get down", Tanya yells at them as she dives behind a tree.

Grabbing Tabrinia and laying down on the ground behind a tree, they hear a thunderous explosion as they lay down. They can feel the sudden rush of hot air enveloping them. As the wind subsides, they get up and look at where the house was. There is nothing left, except a big hole in the ground.

"Hey you guys. We need to get the hell out of here before someone shows up and wants to know what the explosion was. C'mon", Kensing says as he grabs Tabrinia's arm and runs towards the hole where the house used to be.

Tanya follows them as they run. Getting to the hole in the ground, Kensing shakes his head. Just then from out of the doors leading to the lab, they see a bunch of creatures come pouring out of them. "Oh shit", Kensing says as he reaches in his pocket and withdraws a patch.

Ripping the backing off, he slaps it on his arm. Grabbing his gut as the pain comes back to him, he falls to the ground and moans out. Watching in horror as the creatures come from out of the lab, the girls help Kensing as the pain finally subsides. "Thanks", he says as he gets up and starts placing another patch on his arm.

Tabrinia feels in her pocket and takes a patch out. Taking the adhesive plastic off the back, she slaps it on her arm. As soon as the patch is on her arm, the pain starts. Grabbing her stomach, she falls to the ground as she screams out in pain. Looking at her, Kensing knows what is happening.

Guarding her, he keeps the creatures at bay until she recovers and joins him. Standing up, she feels a strength and power she has never felt before. Smiling as she starts pushing the creatures back into the lab, her powers are not fully functional yet. About ten of the creature's escape as they round up the rest of them back into the lab and back into the doorway.

Following the creature's footprints, they find some of them and kill them. Coming back to the house, they tell Tanya, they couldn't get them all. He said there were about two out there still. As they all agree there was nothing they could do, they go back into the lab and turn all the power off. Pulling all the breakers out of the box, Kensing disconnects them.

Leaving the lab, they go out and head towards town. Walking through the woods, they find one of the creatures. Killing it, they bury the body in a remote spot as best they can. Continuing on, they see a bunch of lights go by heading towards the house. Ducking down as they go by, they leave the town by foot.

Watching as the humans leave, the last creature goes into the lab. Trying to start the doorway up, he can't figure out what to do. Hearing a lot of loud whining noises coming closer, the creature goes back outside and hides in the woods. Watching as the humans get out of their vehicles and shake their heads, they don't see anything left. Leaving after looking around and not finding anything, they head towards town.

After the police and fire department leave, the creature goes back down to the lab. It can't figure out what to do. Pushing buttons and pulling levers, nothing happens. Shaking its head, it does whatever it thinks will work. Not having any luck, it finally gives up. Finding a place to hide, the creature stays in hiding. Waiting. Watching. Hoping. Hoping someone comes that can open the doorway.

Watching as the cops and firemen leave, they decide to go back to the lab. Heading back, they don't see anything out of the ordinary. Getting to the lab, they go down. "Well... What do we do now?" Kensing asks the girls.

Shaking her head, Tabrinia says, "I don't know".

"Don't look at me", Tanya replies as she backs up a little.

"We have to do something.... I just don't know what, yet", Kensing says.

Looking around, he doesn't see anything that will help. "It's your choice girls.... We can 1, go give ourselves up to the cops, or 2, we can open the doorway and try to find a place to live there, or 3, we can hitchhike across the states and try to hide away from everyone?" Kensing says.

Not giving them much of a choice, they all agree to open the doorway and see if they could find somewhere else to live. Putting all the breakers back in, he cranks up the generator as they power up the system and then start putting in different figures to see if it will change where it takes you. Opening the doorway up, Kensing goes through and looks around.

Coming back through Kensing says, "Nothing", as he shakes his head.

Closing then opening the doorway again, he goes back through. Not finding anything for a few hours, he finally finds a nice, quiet, peaceful looking place. Coming back through he says, "C'mon let's go. I want you to see this".

As they all go through the doorway, the creature comes from out of hiding and shuts the doorway. Roaring a triumphant cry, it restarts the system. As the doorway opens, the creature goes through and finds the big, badass dude. Showing him that he got the doorway open, they go through and into the lab.

Going through the doorway, they all look and see a beautiful place. Agreeing that this is the place, they turn around and try to go back through the doorway. Stepping where they think it is, they find out they are still in the same place. "What the hell happened?" Kensing asks.

"I don't know", Tabrinia says. "Unless...", she starts to say when Tanya interrupts her.

"I bet it's the last creature. I can almost taste it", Tanya says as she interrupts Tabrinia.

"Could be. Damn", Kensing replies as he hammers his fist into his other hand.

"I guess that's it. They are going to take over the planet. That's how it gets destroyed", Tabrinia says as she looks down at the ground. "And it wasn't Terrin's fault after all. It's our fault".

"Wait a minute... The guy pointed Terrin out as the one who did it", Kensing says.

"Maybe he pointed him out cause he is the one who made the machine", Tabrinia suggests.

"Could be....... Shit..... Now what?" Kensing asks.

Shaking their heads, they offer nothing. Not believing they are stuck here forever no matter what, Tanya starts crying. "Hey, hey, hey...

What's wrong?" Kensing asks as he hugs her.

Shaking her head back and forth, she doesn't say anything. "C'mon Tanya... Talk to me", Kensing begs.

Finally after a few minutes she says, "I miss my family. I have lost everything I have ever loved. I have nothing left", as she starts crying again.

"Wait a minute... You have us", Kensing says. "We don't have anything left either".

Looking up at him she says, "Yeah... That's right", as she tries to smile.

Smiling at her he says, "Now we have to find a way to get back. We can't let hell go to Earth. We made it possible, I think it's our responsibility to make things right again".

"I know what you mean. I feel terrible about this", Tabrinia says.

"How can we get back?" he ponders out loud.

"Didn't you open it one time by using your mind power?" Tabrinia asks as she shrugs. "Maybe we can combine our minds and open it together?"

"Let's try it. Ready?" he asks.

"Ready", she replies.

"Okay. Now", he says, as they think and concentrate on opening the doorway up.

Tanya looks around and sees a shimmering, a few feet away. "Hey... It's working", she says out loud.

Opening their eyes they see the doorway starting to open up. Smiling as the shimmering becomes stable, they walk through and into the lab. But when they get there, they are not ready for what they see when they get there. Stepping through they see the big, badass dude there and a few creatures. They are looking at them with strange expressions on their faces. Roaring all together, Tabrinia, Tanya and Kensing cover their ears.

Getting a patch out of his pocket, Kensing slaps one on and then tries to erect a sound barrier. The sound dwindles away as the shield goes into place. Watching as Kensing put another patch on, Tabrinia takes one out of her pocket and slaps two on. Feeling the rush course through her body, she feels great.

Smiling as she looks at the big, badass dude, she thinks of him shrinking. Watching as the big guy gets smaller, the other creatures look on and then start laughing, (if that's what you could call it). Getting angry as he shrinks, he tries to break their hold. Not succeeding, it starts trying to fling balls of electricity and flame at them.

When they hit the barrier, they dissipate into nothing. "I think maybe you guys made a big mistake", Kensing says. "Now it's our turn to make you do as we wish", as he looks at them and gives them a rather, evil looking grin.

Making them move around in a circle, they get them to where they are in front of the doorway. Powering up the system, they turn it on and then force all the creatures along with the little, badass dude. Laughing as they see the dude so small, he is almost as big as a small chow puppy. When all the creatures are back in their own domain, they close the doorway.

"Okay. Does anyone have any ideas as to

how we can keep the system down without trashing it?" Kensing asks.

"I know", Tabrinia says as she goes over to the computer and says, "Jennifer".

"Yes. May I help you in checking out today", it replies.

"We need you to open the doorway with these figures and then put it on password protect. Must use password to activate. Can you do that?" she asks.

"Activating system and opening doorway. Activating password mode...... Activated... Password required to operate system..... Stand-by...... Doorway is fully open. You have five minutes to go through", the computer says.

"Ready?" Kensing asks the girls.

"I'm ready", Tanya says.

"I'm ready too", Tabrinia replies.

Holding hands, they walk through the doorway. Looking around, they see they are where they wanted to be. Smiling as they go and investigate the world, they walk away from the doorway. As they are walking away from the doorway, a creature comes through and follows them. Walking and holding hands, they explore their New World.

"You know... This is what I would expect the world to be like when Adam and Eve were supposedly alive", Kensing says.

"Yeah... It's a new and different feeling. Like there is no crime here at all", Tanya agrees.

"This is going to be soo much fun", Tabrinia says. "Exploring a New World. I would have never even dreamed of anything like this".

"Yeah... I know what you mean. Well... I guess this is what we will call home from now on", he says as he links arms with the girls.

ABOUT THE AUTHOR;

Terrence Dean Astleford was born on July 28 in Grand Rapids, Michigan. He currently resides in Florida where he continues writing more stories and working.

www.ingramcontent.com/pod-product-compliance
Lightning Source LLC
LaVergne TN
LVHW020541100826
845148LV00010B/1562

* 9 7 8 0 9 8 3 6 7 4 3 2 0 *